Snow of the White Hills

A Gay Fairytale

by

Wendy Rathbone

Dedication

For all my readers!
Thank you so much!
I couldn't keep doing this without you!

A Note to the Reader

This story takes place in a fairytale, pre-industrial, fictional landscape and is not meant to be historically accurate for any known time and place.

Chapter One

A sparrow hopped about on the ledge of the barred window, feathers ruffled in the cool breeze. It slowly approached the crumb Snow had put out for it. Fighting instinctive mistrust, it jumped back and forth, tilting its head, eyeing the bread.

Snow said softly, "I understand. I don't like people, either."

Finally, the sparrow found its moment of bravery and snatched the bread crumb in its tiny black beak. Wings extended. The air softly shuddered.

The sparrow flew with its prize into the misty morning sky.

Snow watched it until it became a dark dot on the horizon and vanished.

He turned back to survey his room. The round ceiling sloped upward to a point at the tip of the castle's tallest tower. Cold rock walls surrounded him, dark and damp. A heavy wooden door leading to a winding, metal staircase took up space on one side. On the other, a hearth dented the wall, empty save for gray silt at its floor.

Snow longed for a fire, and the scent of burning pine or oak. More, he longed for a real life, a free life. But that was not to be had.

His bed lay rumpled to his right. Clean sheets were brought maybe once month, if the guards remembered. He had two threadbare blankets and what might once have been called a pillow, but was now mostly dust encased in old linen.

His clothes were at least two years old by now. The trousers, black, were well-made and wool. They had seen better times but still held up. His shirt on the other hand, was now more yellow than white and had become threadbare, sheer against his chest and arms.

The guards had let him keep his birthday robe. The day he'd turned eighteen, the gift of a fine royal purple robe had been his right.

He'd loved the velvet feel of it. It added warmth on the worst nights of the nine month long winters in the White Hills.

Snow sat on the edge of his bed, waiting. He looked at the pile of books on the floor.

The old lady had never said he could not read to while away the long hours, and so the nicer guards brought books to him.

Against the wall leaned an old wooden table with a broken leg, littered with candle stubs. He had half a candle left in a chipped glass stand, which he was saving. Sometimes, when he asked nicely, the guards remembered to bring him fresh candles. But lately his requests had been ignored.

Snow's breath fogged in front of him. He shivered but was used to it. He was cold all the time. At least he didn't starve. At least he had not gone mad. Yet.

He attributed that to the old lady. He usually had three small meals a day, which he shared with the birds when the weather warmed a little. And the old lady met with him sometimes, coming up to his locked tower room to ask him strange questions such as if he thought she was beautiful. Sometimes she received him in her luxurious royal chamber that connected to the throne room. When she had the guards bring him to her, it was for things other than questions. Snow thought at first she was trying to make a child from him. But that never happened. Still, she took him to her bed. Once a month. And he was not aloud to protest, or speak of it to anyone.

Thus, he had occasional stimulus, even if it was against his will. He was able to see that the palace still ran smoothly, that servants, guards, masters and maids saw to the upkeep and nothing but his own tower prison had fallen to ruin.

When he visited the old lady in chambers, that was the only time he experienced real warmth. Not from her, but from her always blazing hearth stacked neatly with fresh wood, and the hundreds of candles she surrounded herself with.

Always when he visited her, he longed to stay. But only for the heat and comfort. Not for her. He endured her only because she frightened him. He did everything she told him to do, but it was never enough. He obeyed her because he had no choice. And because he wanted to live.

He still dreamed of being free. Even alone, locked in the freezing tower room, he had not lost hope that one day he would find a way out of this life and enter a new world where he did not have to be afraid. Where he could know warmth. Where the intimate touch of a hand on his skin did not make him recoil.

After two years it was amazing, actually. That he could still hope. That he could dream.

Chapter Two

Snow lay back on satins the color of dark blood.

The old lady--who wasn't really all that old but the depth of iciness in her gaze made her look ancient and so Snow had always thought of her that way—surrounded herself with mirrors, and Snow could see in them how white he was against the sheets, and how lean.

His pale hair, straight and soft, reflected the light in stripes of gold. The old lady ran her fingers through it.

"Too long. Needs a trim." Her voice criticized. Always. Always.

Snow was never good enough.

She crouched over him, naked, her small breasts pert and pink. She had her long, golden hair down and it trailed over her shoulders, brushing against his chest.

He wanted to close his eyes but she did not like that. She wanted him to look at her. Wanted him to watch the things she did.

"You are pretty as a girl, but not as pretty as me. Say it." She always commanded him.

"You are beautiful," he said softly. But his mind went elsewhere, to the birds he fed at his window, to his childhood memories of when his father was still alive and the palace was his to roam, his to inherit one day. He'd been well-loved. His father had been a great man.

But the old lady, the queen—not Snow's mother but the second queen who came soon after Snow's mother died—changed all that. Snow had not seen it coming, not had time to adapt, and when his father died just before he turned eighteen, he did not realize she had plans to never let him rule. She secured him in the tower and told the kingdom he had died.

Then she tried to make a child with him. Over and over. For two years.

Now, life was something to endure, not enjoy.

Snow blinked against the mirrored reflections, the candles gold haze, and began to count his breaths. One. Two. Three.

"You lie." Her breath was like roses. A scent he hated.

"You are beautiful, Serena. Everyone knows."

"The most beautiful in all the lands?" she asked.

He looked at her multiplied reflection in several of the mirrors. Her body was probably pretty. He didn't know. He couldn't see her that way. "Yes."

She gave a little grunt and moved down, her gaze raking his front. "Then why aren't you hard?"

Snow swallowed and stared upward at the ornate ceiling hung with colorful tapestries and set his jaw. He knew what would come next and tried to think about a better future.

Her touch was not cold, but the feel was icy. Her mouth on him heated him up, but it was like winter incarnate.

She sucked him until he could not control the response. The motion of her head. The pressure of her tongue. Against his will, his cock hardened.

He didn't want this. It was tantamount to rape. But he had fought her once and lost. Whipped to within an inch of his life. He still bore the scars. The memory of that pain made him cringe.

It was easier to give in. Easier to wait. One day, maybe, he would get away.

He often helped himself respond to her will by pretending she was someone else. One of the handsome guards, perhaps. Or a farmhand with lovely, tanned muscles. He'd always dreamed of men in his erotic fantasies. Probably because the old lady had ruined him for women. He didn't know. All he understood was that his attraction to males in his fantasies helped him to perform for her.

When he was slick enough and hard enough to please her, she straddled him and rode him hard.

This part could last as long as an hour. The old lady could be insatiable. And he was a good partner because he did not always feel his peak with her. She did not arouse him. He could stay hard for hours without any urge to come. Usually, he did come inside her if he focused in on himself and his fantasies, and made it happen. But sometimes he could not climax.

When it first happened—that he could not come—she was offended. She smacked him hard. Then sucked him over and over until he could feel almost nothing. But when it happened a second time, she ignored it. Said nothing. Did nothing.

Today she bounced on him grunting and groaning away, bringing herself to climax after climax, making him lick her afterward and causing another orgasm to shudder through her.

She leaned down toward his face and whispered, hot and rose-scented into his ear. "When you don't come, it makes me think you're getting a little side-action. What is it? A guard? A maid who brings your meals?"

"No, Serena."

"Huh." She crawled off him and stood by the side of the bed, long hair tangled all about her, looking down at him. "I think you should have less contact with people. Only my most trusted guard with a key. Only two meals a day. No books."

He caught his breath. His eyes stung. He lifted himself on one elbow, watching himself reflected triple in the mirrors. "I will come for you, Serena. By my own hand."

"I don't want you to come that way! I want you to fuck me like real man. Something you are incapable of."

His throat tightened at the thought of being more alone than he already was, with no new books. And less food. He was already thin, his ribs showing beneath his pale, thin skin.

His mind desperately searched for another way. "Would you like to try again? I can take you from behind, the way you seem to like it."

"Yes, I do like it. But only if you are sincere. Honest with me. And tell me I am beautiful again and again."

He sat up. "You are beautiful. The most beautiful being in all the land."

"With your pretty face, I'm not so sure." She sneered. "At least everyone thinks you're dead, so there is that."

"I will take you any way you like, beautiful Serena. I promise I will come. Just please let me have my books."

She shrugged, scratching at her groin in a most unbecoming way. "But sweet boy, it's too late. I tire of you. And I'm sore."

Walking naked to her chamber door, the old lady opened it wide, not caring who saw her freshly fucked body, hair knotted, skin shining with sweat.

"Guards, take him away!"

Snow rose, quickly putting on his clothes and his purple robe. He was not allowed shoes. Barefoot, the queen's guard led him away, but not before she'd conferred with the guard that all his books should be removed, and his meals reduced.

Snow followed the guards up the winding staircase. Up and up. To the cold. To the hopeless rock walls and one barred window.

When the door to the tower room banged shut, Snow lowered his head and swallowed back the salt of tears.

Chapter Three

A ghost said to Snow, "Come with me."

It had to be a ghost. For it was the middle of a cold night and the dark form had no face.

"Come with me now!" The ghost had substance, for it shoved him hard on the shoulder.

Snow did not have to dress. The night was so frosty he'd slept in all his clothes, including his robe. With the dirty sheet and both blankets drawn up, still he shivered.

His bare feet stung as they hit the tower room's stone floor.

Snow followed the ghost out the door and down the winding stairs.

Could the old lady want him again so soon? And in the middle of the night?

But as they moved toward the throne room and the connecting private chamber of the queen, they did not stop.

They came to the palace entrance and were met by two of the queen's guard. Snow recognized one as the captain, the queen's most trusted man.

Now, in the dim moonlight shining on snow-packed grounds, Snow could make out the features of his ghost. Dressed in the brown leathers of one of the queen's huntsman, he wore a belt dangling with sheathed knives of varying sizes. The guards all wore their swords.

The three of them jangled as they walked into the deep winter night, boots crunching icy groundcover. All but Snow whose bare feet went quickly numb as he stumbled in the huntsman's grasp through ankle-deep flakes.

Snow came to a halt as he realized he was being taken away from the palace, the only home he'd ever known. Something was more wrong than ever. If he felt it on waking, he knew it now for sure.

"Come on!" the huntsman said, jerking him forward.

"Where are you taking me?" Snow stumbled again as the man yanked his arm.

"No questions!"

The two guards in front turned to watch them.

Snow said, "You can't take me from the palace. I'm the prince!"

"You're no one."

The two guards actually laughed.

"No! I won't go." Snow pulled back, but his strength was no match for the huntsman.

Laughing again, the guards came forward. "Are we going to have to carry him?" said the captain.

Snow pulled free of the huntsman's grasp. Turning, he slipped and fell hard. He could not feel his feet. He could not run.

"Looks like it," said the huntsman.

Snow felt himself yanked hard by the arms. His shoulders nearly dislocated. With great force, he was lifted high and slung over the back of one of the guards. He couldn't see which one.

Snow tried pounding on his back, but the guard only chuckled and the party moved into the deep, dim White Hill woods.

It was then Snow knew for sure, breaths coming uneven. They were going to kill him.

And leave him to the wolves.

*

"The queen showed you pity for two years, and all you did was disrespect her."

Lying in a pile of snow in a clearing after they'd walked for what seemed to be miles, Snow could do nothing to defend himself. He was frozen through. He could not move. And his feet felt like this were broken off, gone.

"The queen is not your true ruler," he said. Snow had had this conversation before with many a guard. To no avail. The old lady had arrived in Snow's childhood with her own wealth. That, combined with the treasure vault of Snow's father, gave her ample enough means to pay her henchmen well. They would do anything for her. Maim. Murder. Even die. All for money.

"The queen is the only ruler of this land."

"This is murder," Snow said. "Regicide. For I am the true king."

"Everyone thinks you died of a fever shortly after your eighteenth birthday," said the huntsman, whose face showed a rictus of scars in the milky, weak moonlight. "There is no regicide. You don't exist."

The guards stood back. Watching.

"If you just let me go, then. Please. I will disappear. I'll never return. She doesn't have to know."

"Then whose heart will I bring to her on a platter to prove to her you are dead?"

Snow felt his body tighten; his jaw ached. The cold made him sluggish. "She asked for my heart?"

"She considered having me bring her your cock."

Snow gulped. The old lady had always been icy, strange. It was madness to have him locked away. Greed for power. He knew that. He even understood it, criminal as that was. But this? It went beyond madness and into pure evil.

"Please don't kill me."

"Sorry lad." The huntsman unsheathed a long knife. It glittered silver, reflecting the paleness of the snow.

The captain of the guard shouted out. "Do you need us for anything further? Or can you handle the rest on your own."

"I'm fine," the huntsman said. "Go back. Tell the queen I will arrive by dawn."

"Very well."

The guards left, crunching down the icy path they had made through the wood.

Maybe, Snow thought, they actually didn't have the stomach to see this through to the end. To watch the huntsman actually butcher their true prince.

Snow was so cold, he was beyond shivering. Beyond feeling. He had the unbidden thought that death would have to be warmer than this. This cruel existence. His life with no hope, no future, no end to dishonor and torment.

He would welcome it, then. His last bed would be red, like the queen's, but not satin, no, it would be soaked in blood on ice. On snow. Like his name. His pale body would wither and become food for the plants and animals of the forest. And his unbeating heart would be placed in the palms of the old lady, who would see it reflected ten times over in all her mirrors, and call herself the most beautiful being in all the land.

14

But in truth, she would be the ugliest. Though no one would ever know, she would know. The old lady would live ugly, reflected on and on in her candle-scented chambers, in her royal evil mind, to the end of her days.

The huntsman bent over Snow and the knife flashed.

Snow swallowed hard. Already his mind was fading. He leaned his head back into the drift. Felt his hair snag on a crystal of ice.

Then he felt a snick of the knife against his chest, a great weight, and darkness.

Chapter Four

The woods were dying. A winter sea of white. Somewhere, voices. Hushed. Or calling. A sparrow chirped. Damp wool's musky scent. Taste of bitter salt. Spiny branches. Sharp pine adrift, causing a green sneeze. Twice.

Snow saw a star floating on the air. A fairy myth.

In the throes of dying, maybe he was hallucinating. Did his heart still beat? Did Snow still even own it?

Another sneeze. Not his own.

Shadows. Boots crushing frosted dew. Bustling coats. Huffs. Breaths.

He could not feel his body. But his vision was upside-down, and the ground jumped forward and back. Over and over. Jiggling him. Juggling him.

He saw dark fur at the edge of his vision where the ground swelled and swayed. Kidnapped by bears, he thought. Bears coming out of hibernation.

They sure smelled like bears. At least his nose still worked. He heard a moan.

"He's coming to!" someone said.

A man answered. "We're almost there." The huntsman? No, this voice was deep. Rich. Relaxed. Not desperate or angry or murderous. This was new.

Snow could do nothing. The bears were taking him wherever bears took their prey. The talking bears. The sneezing bears.

He wanted to laugh. Or cry. He could do nothing but let himself be whisked away to somewhere, to nowhere. Into the unknown.

*

Snow could not lift his head, but when whatever was carrying him turned, he was able to see a line of booted feet and legs. Several bears, or people maybe, surrounded him. They had gone in and out of trees, but here were more trees, gnarled bare branches along with a

16

mix of evergreen. And before them, a swell in the earth like a fairy mound. And indeed, it was something tricky, for in the mound was a door with a brass ring on the handle.

A gloved, furry hand reached down and grasped it. The door pulled back revealing a hole in a hill.

Hands reached out. Snow decided they were touching him, lifting him into that hole, but he could not feel them. He was frozen to numbness.

Down, down they went into darkness, into hell. By the fairy light that still bobbed before him, Snow saw roots in the walls, and little sprigs of white where some of the baby roots escaped the earth. The dirt smelled musty, almost spicy, but the air was fresh, warmer on his cheeks which stung.

"Put him here," said a voice.

"That's my bed," said another.

"Shite, it's the biggest one. You can spare the room."

"The sheets are clean, at least."

A tawny glow filled the air.

Snow blinked, trying to see, but still there were only furry shadows, breathy voices, and darkness trying to impinge on all sides. His head ached. His body felt like an added on bit of weight, nothing more.

His vision came level and he decided he must now be lying on his back. He could see a dark ceiling made of bumpy rock. To his right, something flickered and glowed. A hearth. A fire.

His body wanted to shiver at the thought of that fire but he could not move.

Several large, black shapes surrounded him. He had no strength left to be afraid. He only wondered. What were they? Was this the other side? Life after death?

"Get those clothes off him. They are frozen to his skin and when they start to melt, they'll be soaked."

Hands came out of the shadows, furred, black. A lot of them. He could tell they were moving him, tugging, untying, unbuttoning, peeling. He became afraid that his body was breaking away with the clothing. First the robe was pulled off, then the threadbare shirt, the black trousers. And then he was wearing nothing, but he couldn't see.

Someone said, "Shit."

Someone else, said, "He looks carved from snow itself."

Snow felt a yank at the foot of the bed. His head moved down a little.

A voice said, "I don't know if I can save the feet. Get more furs! Cover him. Hap, you and Sleepy take off your clothes and get in with him. Skin to skin. It's the best way to heat him up again."

No one protested.

Snow closed his eyes and decided he'd gone insane.

Fur covered him head to toe. He opened his eyes enough to see two naked men standing on either side of him. One had skin of night, and dark eyes. He was heavily muscled. The other had hair like shades of autumn, but more medium brown skin. He also looked made of muscle. His smile was wide and pretty.

They both got under the furs with Snow and pulled him against their bodies.

"Heat up the water. I'm going to see what I can do about his feet."

"Right, Doc," said a voice.

Snow shut his eyes again, his headache increasing. The first bit of feeling came at his throat. Tendrils of heat. Breath where a face pressed against the side of his.

Then he felt hands running up and down his cold body. All over he began to shiver so hard he couldn't keep still. His muscles cramped up and down his legs, arms and torso.

Snow moaned. Gasped. He suddenly felt as if he could not breathe.

"Easy," said the darker man. He reached up and brushed the hair from Snow's cheek. Then he leaned over him, his body hot and hard-muscled against Snow's side. "Hey, Sleepy, wake up!"

The other man with the pretty smile grunted. "He's like being in bed with a giant icicle. I'm not asleep, Hap, I'm concentrating on thawing him."

"Put your leg over his."

"Yeah. He's so cold all over. How is he alive?"

Snow cried out. The shivers were like convulsions. Everything hurt. Luckily, his feet were still numb.

Sleepy said, "You'll be fine. It hurts at first. I know."

That was no comfort. Maybe later, Snow could comprehend the words, but now all he wanted to do was escape the pain.

Doc said, "His feet are so swollen. I'm going to have to make some cuts."

Snow, in his dim haze, felt himself try to surface. He flailed. "Please don't cut off my feet."

And then he was drowning again, as if in a fever. But made of ice. And more ice. Ancient and old, never having seen a ray of sun.

Something stung him by his feet. He began to yell.

A man approached the bed, holding out a ceramic cup. "See if you can get him to drink this."

"What is that? Rum?" asked Sleepy.

"Yes."

"How'd you know I need a drink? Give it to me."

"It's for him, idiot."

Someone lifted his head. Hot, stinging liquid poured into his mouth. Snow choked and coughed, but managed to get a few swallows down. He was awake enough to know it would help.

His feet began to ache, then pound as if someone was cutting them off.

Snow yelled again.

"More rum. Get as much down him as you can."

Snow coughed some more. His eyes were streaming, his freezing cheeks wet.

A gentle hand petted his hair. He thought of the old lady telling him he needed a trim. Telling him he was a pretty boy but not as pretty as she.

But this hand was different, not rough, not critical. It soothed. A voice in his ear crooned. The one they called Sleepy. "Try to sleep. You'll be warmer when you wake. We'll be here. We have you. We have you safe now."

He was surrounded on all sides by bodies, voices, and none were trying to hurt him, but still all he felt was pain.

He yelled again and again. Into the bleak air, into the darkness underground.

Finally, he passed out.

Chapter Five

Snow dreamed of fire and ice, earthen rock walls and faraway voices.

He opened his eyes and saw the room about him a wavering daze.

Something made a strange, muffled low buzz in his ear. He turned his head and realized a man lay with his head on his shoulder snoring. The man had brown hair and a strong jaw. He remembered him. Sleepy. He had the pretty smile.

As Snow assessed himself, he realized another weight lay atop him on his other side. Hap. A dark arm, well-muscled, curved about Snow's chest.

Snow stretched himself, feeling his muscles want to cramp. It was awful. But also good. He could feel again. His body was his. His heart still beat inside his chest.

What had happened?

His feet burned. He could not wiggle his toes. Something heavy was on them. He wanted to ask, to look, but everything was so still and quiet. Where was he? What was all this?

He slowly lifted his head.

To his right, a hearth-fire merrily burned. In front of it sat a long wooden table. Out of place in the dark, in the deep of winter, stood a crystal vase of red flowers. Not roses, which Snow hated. But something else. A winter flower. Poinsettias?

A stack of dishes sat to one side, along with cutlery. Seven ale cups lined the edge of the table. He was sure of it. He counted them twice.

Seven cups for seven people. That meant this must be their home. They lived here. And they really were people, not talking bears.

Snow shifted his body again, and Hap stretched alongside him, shifting as well, letting out a soft, contented sigh.

Sleepy kept snoring away, undisturbed.

Feeling suddenly flushed, and too warm for the first time in years, Snow pushed his arms beneath him and tried to sit up, mindful of the two men on either side. The furs were heavy, but a few slid down baring his chest. Sleepy's head turned and he buried his face in the pillow. Hap shifted just enough to make some room for Snow to move.

He looked down to make sure he had no open wound, that his heart was still within. He remembered the huntsman's knife, and feeling the snick of the blade against his chest, but there was no mark save a small bruise just below his nipple at the curve of his pectoral muscle.

Something had stopped the huntsman from his final crime. Some*one*. He remembered feeling a weight on his body, then— nothing.

"Ah, I see someone has wakened," said a soft voice to his right. He had not seen the man sitting in a chair near the hearth. He had something in his lap. A pile of knitting maybe. Or a cat. Or both.

Snow turned. The figure in the chair wore wire-rimmed glasses. His hair was blond with silver at the edges, but he was not old. He had on a short sleeved muslin tunic that showed his arms. Firm. Muscled.

Snow cleared his throat. "Thank you for helping me."

"My boy, we could not stand by and watch that man murder you."

"But you don't even know me. I thank you for coming to my aid."

"Well, it has been a Sunday of terrible ravens, but one good thing came out of it. We have a new friend."

Snow pressed his lips together in an almost smile. He didn't quite feel up to a real smile yet. "I haven't heard that phrase before. A Sunday of terrible ravens."

"My gran used to say strange things. I picked up a lot of her terms. Let's just say, we had a hard day ourselves. Harassed by the queen's guard when we went to town for supplies. They only let us go because they took every coin we had, claiming we hadn't paid the new tax."

"A new tax?" Snow asked.

"Nothing to concern yourself with now. You need to heal. How do your feet feel?"

"They hurt." Snow swallowed hard. "You didn't cut them off."

Now Doc stood. It was indeed a cat in his lap. A gray one. It landed on its feet, shook its ruffled fur, and slinked off to curl up on a rag rug by the fire.

"I had to take the very tips of the little toes. I'm sorry. They were not coming back to life no matter how hard I tried."

Snow winced, then nodded, holding his feelings in. It could have been far worse, he told himself. He could be without a heart. And dead.

"I also had to make cuts to release the pressure of the swelling. But you should heal fine from those. You will walk again."

Snow brought his arms tight across his chest and nodded.

"Your men—are they your brothers? These two?" Snow asked.

Doc came over to the bed. "No. But they are very dear to me. They've kept you warm."

"I can't repay—"

"Tut-tut. No talk of that. You must rest. Are you thirsty? Hungry?"

Snow felt his cheeks flush. "I think I have to pee."

"I will bring you the chamber pot."

When Doc returned, he tapped Sleepy on the shoulder. "Hey. Sleepy. Hap. Give the guy some privacy, will you? He's warm now."

Hap sat up abruptly. "What just happened?" He looked around the room, then over his shoulder at Snow. "Oh, yeah. Now I remember. How are you feeling, beautiful?"

Snow bit down on his lower lip.

"Ease up on him a bit," Doc said.

"Well, fuck me. I say it. You think it. He is cute." Hap stretched his long, firm arms over his head. They turned copper in the firelight. Then he got up in his altogether, as if he didn't even notice he had not a stitch on, and walked while still leisurely stretching toward the fire. "Coffee?" he asked.

"I made it an hour ago," Doc replied.

Naked, Hap grabbed a cup from the table, bent to the kettle over the fire, and gave everyone who bothered to look a great view of his very firm and lovely rump.

Snow let the air out of his lungs very slowly.

Sleepy sat up, pushing his wavy brunet locks from his eyes. His smile was like a lamp unto itself. Bright as a rising sun. He, too, got up undeterred by his nakedness. "Save some for me," he said to Hap, grabbing his cup from the table.

The two men naked by the fire were a sight. Snow tried to politely look away, but it was difficult. Their bodies were like sculpted marble.

As Snow looked about, he saw glass lanterns with candles hanging about the room. One large lamp hung over the long, wooden table. Shadows stretched on the rock walls and ceiling.

Doc handed Snow a porcelain chamber pot. It looked brand new. Clean. It had a scattering of blue flowers around the rim. Then Doc brought a freestanding curtain to the side of the bed—muslin in a wooden frame on a neatly made stand.

"You will walk again, but you should not try to stand for a few days. Bed rest for you, and all will be well."

Snow sat up and felt the iron frame of the headboard press against his back. He tried to see beyond the frame. He felt space there. Open. Airy. He thought he heard breathing and little snores. Of course there had to be more beds in this underground home. Enough for seven men.

The light had dimmed as the curtain enclosed him half-way. He quickly used the pot and then set it to the side of the bed on the floor, pushing it underneath.

He lay back, exhausted from doing that one chore.

Doc showed up at the edge of the curtain, peering at him. "Would you like some hot coffee? Or we have tea?"

"Yes, tea please."

Doc moved the curtain back so Snow could see the hearth and table again. Hap and Sleepy had, in that short time, managed to put on trousers but nothing more. Hap's were undone at the waist.

Sleepy came over and handed Snow one of the seven cups. Snow could not help but think he was taking something valuable from these men. One of their cups. Tea. A bed. And Doc had offered food. He'd already mentioned they'd been low in supplies and had come from town empty-handed.

Doc brought Snow a plate with warm bread dripping in golden butter.

"But aren't you short on supplies?" Snow asked.

"We like to stockpile. Don't you worry a thing about it."

Hap chuckled, and came over to sit on the edge of the bed, watching Snow take a sip of the tea. It was sweet. Hot. Perfection. He had never tasted anything so good and his stomach growled.

Hap said, "When you feel like eating more than bread, we have a locker full of fresh meat."

"How? I thought you were starving or something," Snow said.

Hap shrugged. "There are seven of us. We all contribute with our talents."

"You all live here?"

"Yes. It works out just right," Hap said. "We all compliment each other very well. We all work several days a week in the quarry to earn coin. We made this home for ourselves just as we want it. Comfortable. Private. Hidden."

"Are you hiding?"

Doc stepped in. "Some of us have had difficult pasts. Now. Eat up. We have honey if you'd like it."

Snow felt as if that was asking too much. Slowly, he shook his head.

When he'd finished eating his bread, which was soft and fresh and hot as if just baked, the butter rich and glowing, he noticed other men enter the kitchen area for coffee. Seven in all. He'd have to learn their names at once. He wanted to know the names of those who'd risked their own lives to save his. Never would he allow himself to forget any of them.

Doc took his plate and cup. "Now rest up, son. You need to heal."

"My name is Snow," Snow replied, scooting down in the bed. His feet felt huge. He realized they were tightly wrapped in thick cloth.

One of the men at the hearth with pale brown hair turned. He sneezed hard. "Damn my body hates mornings."

"Your body hates all times of the day, Sneezy," a blond man said, cocking his hip. His eyebrows narrowed, giving him a sternly annoyed look.

Sneezy ignored the quip. He stared at Snow. "Snow? Like Prince Snow of the White Hills who died of a fever two years ago?"

Snow glanced down at the furs over his legs. "Yes, but of course I'm not he."

"No." Doc said. But there was a knowing in his eyes, as if he already decided Snow lied. "How could you be? He's dead."

Snow said nothing.

"Well, we're glad you're alive," said Hap.

Sneezy took a tentative step forward. "How'd you get those scars on your back?"

"Where are you from?" asked the annoyed blond.

"Why was that huntsman trying to kill you?" asked Sleepy, rocking back in a chair at the table.

Two more men, yawning, joined the party, grabbing cups for coffee. But they were one cup short.

Hap held out his cup to the final one, a copper-haired man with a long, proud nose, the tallest of the bunch. "Here, Dope. Use mine. I've had enough coffee for a while."

"We'll have to get another cup."

"Already planned to go to town this afternoon, Bash," Hap said.

"It's Monday. We have to work."

"I'll take off early. You can join me if you want."

"It'll mean a cut in our pay."

Snow felt sorry that he could not pitch in. But then no one had asked him to. He needed to get well first. And besides, no one had even invited him to stay.

"So?" Sleepy said, staring at him with soft brown eyes. "What happened to you? The scars on your back look deep. And where in hell did you come from? Are you going to answer our questions?"

Snow was not good at lying. He froze, eyes wide.

"Now, now, don't overwhelm him. He needs more time to rest," Doc admonished.

"I—I will answer." But Snow knew his identity as the prince might endanger them all. He couldn't tell them. And until he got on his feet, he needed to hide here for as long as he could.

"Just a farm boy. I'm nobody. The huntsman once worked for my father and felt cheated. He took me to get back at him."

"Well, then, we'll return you to your rightful home as soon as possible," Doc said.

Snow nodded. "Thank you. But the huntsman will be searching for me."

"Well," Doc said slowly, "let's just say that won't be a problem."

Several of the men looked at Doc with raised eyebrows.

Sleepy said, "He wasn't dead when we left him." He paused. "Was he?"

The others all looked away from him.

Doc said, "Don't worry. If he did survive the night and the wild wolves, he won't find you as long as you're with us, son."

Who were these men? These seven beautiful saviors? Snow thought if this was a dream, he never wanted to wake.

His body shivered. His headache had diminished but still remained.

Feeling a little chilled again, Snow scrunched under the furs.

"Still, feeling tired?" Doc asked.

"Yes."

"Sleep well," Sleepy said, petting his brow.

Doc added, "Now you all stay hushed. Don't disturb him."

Snow closed his eyes and fell to sleep among friendly warmth and whispers.

Chapter Six

A soft grip on his upper arm brought Snow from his slumber.

Doc, his spectacles shimmering in the firelight, said in a soft voice, "We have to work today. I've left you lunch on a small table here by your bed. Venison, fresh bread, some cheese. And a pitcher of water. The candle in the lantern is new. It should burn all day. But there's an extra in the little drawer underneath this table."

Snow pushed himself up on his elbow. "Thank you."

"Do you read?" Doc asked.

"Yes."

"I expect you'll sleep the day away. You need it. But if you find yourself awake, I've left a book of stories here as well by the tray. They have entertained all of us on cold, long winter nights."

Snow allowed a half-smile to stretch his lips.

"We'll be back by sundown. You're safe here. The door will be locked. Only we have the keys. If you don't think you'll be all right alone, I can take a day off. But we all really need to work after the queen's guard took our coin yesterday. It wasn't all we had, but it does deplete us. We have already lost work days due to blizzard conditions. It's been a hard winter. No work. No pay. You understand."

Snow nodded. "I'll be fine."

"Are you in pain? I can leave the rum by your bedside, too."

Snow's feet did hurt, but he didn't want to take more. Already, the men's hospitality had been generous. "I'll be fine," Snow repeated.

Doc sighed. "All right, then. I'll change your bandages on your feet when we return. The healing will take time. But you'll walk again soon."

"Thank you for everything." Snow looked up to see other faces behind Doc peering at him. "All of you. Tonight I want to learn all your names."

Hap came forward. "Just rest, beautiful." He patted Snow on the top of the head.

The word made Snow tense for a moment. He heard the old lady's voice in his mind.

Tell me I'm the most beautiful in all the land.

But he was safe. She could not find him here. She could not hurt him anymore.

Snow settled back in bed as he watched the men file through the up-sloping hall that led to the door in the ceiling—the ground.

Dark sleep claimed him when he closed his eyes.

*

Snow slept for hours. What woke him was pain. His feet blazed as if they were on fire.

He breathed in deep. The air smelled fresh, as if there was a hidden air vent somewhere in the ceiling/ground. The hearth blazed low. It was banked with coals to keep it going all day.

Snow moved his feet to try to ease the burn, but it only worsened.

He looked at the food on the bedside table but could not bring himself to eat. The pain made him nauseated. All he could do was lie as still as possible and try to endure.

After what felt like an hour or more, he longed for a cup of rum to help him relax and regretted telling Doc he'd be fine without it.

He spied the jar on the table, eyed the distance he'd have to travel to get it, and decided he could make it just fine on his hands and knees.

He pushed the heavy furs aside. His naked body greeted him, white and lean. He looked down at his feet which were like two white balls. They'd been wrapped tight around and around with strips of linen. They looked odd, as if they should not be a part of him anymore, and the pain radiated from them up through his body in agonizing waves.

He rolled off the bed, catching himself on his hands and knees. He was weaker than he realized, and his feet hit the floor with a bump. The pain made him see red and white flashing lights behind his eyes, and he thought he might pass out.

Slowly, he regained his senses and began to crawl toward the table.

On a bench against one wall sat the silver cat. It watched him with a grave, green stare.

By the time he reached the closest end of the table, he was covered in sweat and thoroughly exhausted. He raised himself up on his knees, and his feet touched the floor, again sending arrows of pain through his legs and up into his hips and abdomen. His lungs caught. His throat tightened.

He reached for the bottle of rum and a cup. Shakily, he poured. Some of it spilled but at least he got himself a cupful. He drank some, then refilled the cup. The warmth of the rum ran down his throat and into his stomach creating a comfort that began to extend throughout his body.

Setting the re-filled cup on the floor, Snow knelt, concentrating on keeping his burning feet up off the floor, then slowly made his way back to bed pushing the cup in front of him. When he got to the bed, he set the cup on the bedside table. Then he crawled back up into the bed trying to use his knees for leverage. He slipped and his feet banged against the floor again.

He cried out. He hoped he hadn't done them more damage.

Finally, back in bed, he lifted the rum to his lips again and drank. He saw the cat jump down from the bench and up onto the big table. There, she lifted on paw and began to lick it.

Slowly, the strong drink sank through Snow's body, and his mind whirled. His feet still hurt, but he no longer cared. The feeling the rum left him with was like being encased in warmth, safety and pleasure.

Soon, he was back to sleep.

*

A happy whistling tune woke him. Then voices.

Snow lifted his head and opened his eyes.

"I see he got to the rum," said the copper-headed guy. Dope, they'd called him, Snow recalled. He looked to be the youngest of the bunch.

"You didn't eat your lunch," Doc said, coming to his side.

"Not hungry," Snow replied, wiping the sleep from his eyes.

Seven men surrounded him. Seven heroes. Seven friends.

He saw that Hap carried a pack of goods, followed by Bash with another pack. They set their bags on the table and began to sort through them. Snow was happy they'd gotten to town and back with no trouble. Relieved their supply run had been a success.

They all seemed fresh-eyed and strong after a long day at work. He couldn't imagine that sort of job. A quarry involved hard work, digging for rocks, splitting rocks, lifting rocks. No wonder they all had muscles and firm bodies.

Snow would buckle doing that sort of hard labor after only a few hours. He'd had very little exercise cooped up for two years in the tower room of the palace. His skin was firm and young, pretty, even, but his muscles were nothing compared to these men.

Doc went over to survey the new supplies. He smiled. "We'll eat like kings tonight."

He turned to look at Snow.

Snow nearly recoiled at the word *kings*. For truthfully, he was a prince, a king in fact, since his father had died and he'd come of age at eighteen.

But the old lady had had other plans.

Now that he was thinking clearly, he had more questions, but they seemed impolite. For one, it looked as if Hap and Bash had made it to town and back with supplies in one afternoon. If so, then why were all seven men out in the woods in the middle of the night when Snow was almost murdered?

He was grateful, but he now realized that he was not the only one with secrets.

Doc said, "Do you think you can eat a good stew? And we have fresh preserves from last summer. Strawberry."

Snow's stomach growled. The rum had worn off, but his feet burned slightly less, now. "Yes," he replied.

"Excellent."

Snow was amazed as he watched the seven men work as one smooth team. Two volunteered to cook. Two set the table. Two more put the new supplies in cupboards. Doc swept the floor.

The cat got up from its spot on the hearth and jumped up on the table, deciding it was her time to eat as well. The big, strong men became like children with the cat, cooing at her, giving her gentle pats, rubbing the base of her tail which made her arch and stick her tail straight up.

They called her Sil. "Short for Silver," Sleepy informed him with his usual smile.

Sleepy put a small plate of venison on the ground for her. She jumped off the table and began to eat.

Soon a warm bowl was placed in Snow's hands. He wondered whose bowl he was using, and whose spoon, but all the men seemed to be eating so he decided not to worry.

The stew was thick with gravy and chunks of meat, potato, carrots and peas. His first bite made his saliva glands ache—it was so good.

"We call it miner's stew," Doc offered.

"It's wonderful."

"Bread?" Doc offered him a buttered roll on a small, soft cloth.

"Thank you."

When Snow finished the meal, he could not recall having ever had a better one, even from the King's cooks in the palace kitchens when he was young.

"Now we need to see to replacing the bandages on your feet." Doc looked up, the lenses of his glasses flaring red. "Hap, another small cup of rum, please, for our guest."

"I don't think—I wouldn't want to drink it all," Snow stuttered.

The copper-headed Dope guffawed. "You don't think the one bottle is all we got, do ya?"

The others joined in the laughter.

Sleepy, with his slow, sweet smile, brought Snow a cup.

Doc pushed the furs back from Snow's feet, scratching at his thick, gold-gray hair. "Hmm, this will be uncomfortable to say the least. Drink up."

Snow nodded, putting the cup to his lips, feeling the rum warm him all the way down and through his limbs.

Sleepy sat beside him. Snow liked the way the man smelled, like a fresh bough of pine. And that smile against such a chiseled jaw. He wanted to touch his wavy brown hair so badly his fingers twitched.

Sleepy seemed to sense Snow's acceptance of him and moved closer. "I think maybe you should look over here while Doc takes care of your feet. A final introduction all around, perhaps? We haven't done that yet."

"Not real names," said the man by the fire whose brows were so often narrowed in annoyance.

"Shut up, Grump," said Bash, ducking his head.

"Nicknames, of course. The names we all go by. Snow needs to know what to call us, doesn't he?"

Sleepy turned to Snow.

Snow nodded, holding tight to his cup of rum.

"I'm Sleepy, as you probably picked up. They call me that because I love to sleep in. I hate getting up early. On work days, sometimes the others have to drag me out of my bed." He chuckled.

Snow felt Doc begin to unwrap his feet.

"Nice to meet you, Sleepy."

One by one, the others came forward. The brown man who'd held him all night along with Sleepy said, "I'm Hap. They say I have a jolly personality. Happy."

Snow smiled at him, loving the way he moved, so graceful, so strong and effortless.

"That's Bash," said Hap. "He has this habit of talking to the floor. Bashful, I say."

Bash smirked but nodded. Then he gave a little wave of his hand to Snow. He had straight brown, shoulder-length hair, lighter than Sleepy's hair, and soft features. Truly pretty.

Another brunet stepped forward. "They call me Sneezy. Truly, it's allergies, that's all. But oh well. I hate it."

Snow nodded to him as one of the bandages tugged, sticking to his left foot. As Doc peeled it away, it began to burn. He concentrated on breathing evenly.

The copper blond boy came forward. "Dope. When these guys found me, I was in bad shape. I can't remember my childhood. I couldn't read or write or even add one plus one. They didn't tease me about it, just patiently taught me. I called myself Dopey. They shortened it to Dope." He shrugged.

"And of course I'm always last," said the man closest to the fire. He had been poking at it with a tong. "So what if I whine a little at, well, everything! Life is hard. If anyone tries to say otherwise, they're lying. So they call me Grump. I don't care. It doesn't matter. No one will remember me in a hundred years anyway."

The others laughed. Hap gave him a kind slap on the back. "We love ya anyway."

Snow ran it all through his mind, placing faces with names. It was easy because their nicknames fit each man's personality, how he talked, moved or looked.

His feet felt hot and big. He wanted to forget them. He wanted to be well so he could pay these men back. He'd learn to cook the miner's stew. He'd clean. They were so kind, he'd do just about anything to show them how grateful he was.

Doc finished unwrapping the bandages and said, "You're very swollen, but I don't see anymore black like the color your little toes were. Those wounds at the tips of your toes are covering over nicely. But you will be in pain. There's still a lot of healing to happen here. You might have fevers that come and go. We'll watch you carefully, and leave you everything you need while we're gone."

"Thank you, Doc."

"I'll need to treat the cuts again. It will hurt. Sleepy, maybe hold his hand?"

"My pleasure."

Snow felt self-conscious about the touch, but also well-cared for. He was a complete stranger and these men had welcomed him like a brother. But Sleepy was the one he was most attracted to, the sort who peopled his fantasies when he thought that way, when the old lady threatened him if he didn't perform for her in bed.

The treatment hurt and Snow squeezed Sleepy's hand.

"Sorry," he apologized. "It—I didn't mean—"

"I'm pretty strong." That smile! "Squeeze away. I think I can handle it." Then Sleepy reached out with his free hand and brushed Snow's hair from his eyes. "Your hair is so light. Like corn silk from the summer lands."

Snow took a deep, pained breath. "I got it from my father's side—" Then he stopped.

The King of the White Hills had been known for his pure snow-colored hair. He'd named his son Snow because the babe had been born with his father's hair. Now, as he'd grown up, it had darkened a little, with streaks like spun gold.

If these men knew that about the king, they might guess who Snow really was so he didn't want to say any more. Hiding his identity was an instinct; he didn't want to put these men in more danger than they already might be from rescuing him.

"The curls on the ends of my hair are from my mother," said Sleepy.

Despite the pain in his feet, Snow smiled. He liked Sleepy's curls. His brown hair shone in the firelight, the strands a mixture of bronze, honey, and dark brown.

Doc worked quickly applying the stinging balm to Snow's injured feet. A couple of times, Snow tried to pull away.

Doc said softly, "I know, I know. Try to stay still."

Snow wouldn't look at what Doc was doing. Instead, he focused on Sleepy. "Tell me something," Snow said, his body tense and trembling. "Tell me how you came to be here."

Sleepy looked up at Doc and his eyes held a question. Then he looked back at Snow, lips pressed together. He blinked twice, the muscles around his dark eyes tightening.

"Well, these guys are my friends and--" He seemed at a loss for words.

Snow looked around at the others in the front room. Had he asked too much too soon?

Hap stood from the dining table and came over to the side of the bed. "I think maybe we all have certain reasons for being here, like you, Snow. And secrets we keep for safety's sake." His eyebrows rose. "Am I right?"

Snow nodded. His body jerked as Doc began to re-wrap his feet.

"There," said Doc. "Done." He covered Snow's feet with the edge of the furs.

"I'm grateful to all of you," Snow said. "However you all came to be here in this strange and wonderful home-cave is my fortune. I never meant to intrude into your personal lives."

"You haven't," Sleepy said, frowning at Hap. "I want to tell you this, at least. When I had no one left, these men became my friends. When the old king ruled, it was a better life. But the queen died and a new queen came and everything changed."

Snow saw Doc give Sleepy a warning look and shake his head once.

Sleepy pretended he didn't see. "So—that's it. Life is hard. We banded together to make a safe place, pooling our talents. Hap cooks a mean stew. Bash and Sneezy cook, too, and sew. Grump is a great hunter with the bow and arrow. Until I became homeless, I myself was training a few days in town to be a silversmith. But there's not much call for that here. Dope's the son of a carpenter. Doc sees we're all well. We share the chores. We work. Everything you see around you, we made. We cut wood, do laundry. Just like anybody. But sharing makes it all easier. We're warm, we don't starve and we've found companionship in each other."

Stretching his body, now that his feet weren't being prodded or touched, Snow felt suddenly exhausted.

"It's like a dream I've wished on for two years," he murmured. Snow closed his eyes tight, trying not to see the dusty, cold tower room, or think about how alone he'd been. He was too afraid this was really all a dream and he'd wake there in the dark, hopeless and afraid.

"Us? Your wish?" he heard Hap ask.

"Yes."

"Was it so bad where you came from?" Sleepy asked.

Without opening his eyes, Snow replied, "The huntsman came to kill me. There's a reason. He'll be hunting me still."

"Never fear. We'll protect you," Doc said.

"Yes. Yes," came voices from about the room.

Snow managed a small smile, but already sleep was claiming him. He whispered just before the dark embraced him, "I wish I could be one of you and stay, cut wood, sew, cook, split rocks in the quarry…" His voice trailed off.

The bed moved as Sleepy edged closer to him, still holding his hand.

Snow slept.

Chapter Seven

In the darkness, Snow's eyes opened just a crack to see the orange embers of the hearth fire banked low.

Surrounded by rock walls and ceiling, and a stone and earth floor, nothing from the outside world seemed to exist. Just silence but for the occasional soft snapping of the fire.

Brown shadows shivered against the floor and walls. The air nibbled coldly at his nose and one exposed hand.

Beneath the furs lay warmth, comfort, safety. He stretched a little and realized he wasn't alone. Someone was curled against his back. By the pine scent and warm touch, he could tell it was Sleepy. The man had taken a quick liking to him, and Snow loved it for he'd been alone too long. The old lady and her guards had been unfriendly when he did rarely see or speak with them, the queen herself a nightmare come to life.

He shivered at the mere thought of her.

Sleepy's breaths hitched and he moved closer to Snow's back as if sensing his distress without waking.

Snow breathed in, the air cold in his lungs. He could feel Sleepy's nakedness against his own unclothed body, and thought of it as surprisingly natural. Wonderful, in fact. The intimacy of physical contact, after so long with only the old lady's cruelty touching him like an abrasion, made his skin tingle in little currents of pleasure.

He'd always wanted a closeness with someone, anyone, in this way. A brother. A best friend. A male lover.

He had been alone growing up. The other children in the palace were servants and for some reason kept away from him. He'd had a few playmates, but over the years no real long-term friends. And no lovers save the queen, and she didn't count because her idea of lovemaking was threats, intimidation and rape.

Snow felt Sleepy's hand, a gentle weight on his waist. He lifted his own hand and interlocked their fingers.

For a moment, he hesitated in keeping his hand there. He had the sudden thought that maybe this wasn't what he might hope— closeness for the sake of closeness—and that Sleepy was not only doing a duty by keeping him warm, but, simply, there was no other place for him to sleep. He remembered when he'd arrived someone had said this was Sleepy's bed. If all the other's had their own beds, where else would Sleepy rest?

Snow's heart sped up with worry. More anxious thoughts crowded their way into his mind.

Was the huntsman still alive and looking for him? What about the queen's guard? Would Snow ever be able to return home without fear for his life and claim his rightful place on the throne?

He had tried to maintain hope while living as a prisoner in the tower room. He had hoped a faction of guards might overthrow the queen's most loyal guards. But the old lady had everyone too afraid to breathe, to live. And apparently the kingdom under her rule was not a nice or safe place to be anymore. Doc, Sleepy and Hap had alluded to that in more ways than one.

The shadows tumbled along the edges of the table and the floor. The fire sparked. Snow thought if he could stay here, everything might end up being all right. But would these men allow it?

He didn't know. He could not presume anything about them even if they had been his personal heroes in rescuing him from the huntsman.

The fire smelled of cedar and oak. The red flowers on the table had not faded; they glowed like a bright moment when longing leads to a visible dream.

Snow had dreamed of these men. He'd wished for them. Maybe not in specific stance, attributes or attire. But he had pleaded with the notion of all possibilities that some group might deny the queen and fight their way to free Snow from his prison.

It had happened. Just not the way he envisioned.

A whisper surrounded him. For a moment he thought he'd drifted into dream. But then he realized Sleepy was murmuring, hushed and low.

"I sense you're awake. Are you all right? Do you need anything?"

"Thank you, Sleepy, no."

"Bad dreams?"

Snow shut his eyes. Swallowed. His lips parted. He drew in the cold air. Like a hiss of long held back despair, he finally answered. "Yes."

He caught his breath. Waited for his own tension to fade.

Sleepy caught him tighter against him. "I used to have them, too. But I learned to go into my mind and look for something nice. What do you love?"

"I used to love my mother and father but they're both gone."

"No, something here and now. Something not so sad."

"The sparrows that used to sit on my window ledge. I fed them bread crumbs."

"Wonderful," Sleepy said, breath warm against Snow's ear. "A generous and beautiful vision. Keep it with you. Let the sparrow be your sigil. Think of him whenever you are frightened or sad or in pain."

"Thank you, Sleepy."

Snow closed his eyes. Sleepy's fingers folded against his own so they held hands under the covers against Snow's side. He could feel the hard muscles of the man press his back and thighs.

Maybe things could stay like this. Maybe he would never have to go out into the bad world again.

*

It was early, but something rattled at the hearth.

Snow rubbed his eyes. Sleepy still nestled, strong and warm, against him under the furs.

Doc was at the fire adding more logs. He took a metal pail of warmed water off the hook and replaced it with another.

Two men, Dope and Grump, were shirtless and began to wash. It was a lovely scene, calm and ordinary, and they were beautiful men, their musculature gleaming as they washed with the warmed water.

The cat, Sil, sat on the wooden bench along one wall and gracefully groomed as well.

In the darkness toward the back of the underground home, where Snow had not yet seen, he heard stirrings of men rising. And something else.

Breaths. Whispers. Sighs. Muffled moans.

At first he thought one of them might be sick. Or maybe Sneezy was ready to have another one of his allergy attacks.

But it kept up. A voice hissed, "Yes!" And there was a long, drawn-out moan followed by a series of "ohs." And other sounds. Like slurping, wet and slick.

"My turn," someone whispered. "Turn around."

He could hear it all now, clear through the darkness, and ignoring the activities at the hearth, Snow focused.

More little moans.

"Suck it right like that," came a breathy, low voice.

Bash? Snow wondered. Hap? Sneezy? Or maybe all three.

He knew without a doubt now what they were doing. And that he had heard three voices.

Three?

His skin burned at the thought.

Sleepy woke himself with a sweet snore, body jerking. He lay quiet for a few moments.

The noises from the darkness were muffled but obvious.

"Mornin'. Pay that no mind," Sleepy whispered, then backed up out from under the covers.

He came around the bed and stood naked, running his hands up and down his arms. "Brr. Cold! Got more hot water, Doc?"

Doc said, "Over here."

Sleepy moved toward the hearth and Snow's eyes almost burned from gazing at him. He was beautiful, light brown skin, graceful, hard muscles, and a sweet morning erection that swung up and down as he walked. He seemed unaware of it, or perhaps he simply paid it no mind. All over, he was a lovely sight.

Snow could not look away as Sleepy grabbed a rag and unabashedly began to wash himself before the light of the newly fed fire.

The light flamed about the room as Sleepy washed. Dope and Grump had finished bathing and were shouldering into their shirts. Also, they had not been totally nude.

Dope gave Sleepy an askance look, but then set about rummaging for food.

The noises in the other part of the household did not let up for some time. Groans and moans, sweet and low.

Snow was amazed, as if this was all normal, all part of their daily routine. He envied it. He felt his skin burn, and his cheeks grew hot.

Sleepy lazily ran the cloth all over his body.

Doc put more water on the hook over the fire to heat up.

Grump helped Dope get supplies onto a counter. "Porridge again?" he asked.

Dope nodded. "What? You love it."

"It's fine."

Sleepy took handfuls of water and scrubbed at his pretty hair until it was damp, the tendrils teasing his neck and the tops of his shoulders.

Snow could not help but wonder that Sleepy's show of washing right out in the open was partly for him. He wished it was so.

He wished for normalcy, domesticity, a feeling of kin.

These men had it.

No matter their secrets and their pasts, the moment here and now was sublime. He would take Sleepy's advice and think about nice things when he felt bad. The sparrow. Yes. But also this moment. Hearing the sweet whispers and moans behind him in the dark, and seeing Sleepy's beauty come to life before him, damp and glistening in the firelight, taut skin, pretty hands and eyes and face, hair trying to clutch at naked shoulders, and a cock lovely as flower turning to the sun.

It was a shame such beauty had to be covered when Sleepy finally began to dress in his black trousers and muslin shirt.

Doc moved off to feed the cat, his glasses flickering from the firelight. She swished her tail at him, and flirted.

He set her plate down on the bench and she began to eat. He ran his hand down her back and she arched in pleasure, but never stopped eating.

Quickly, Dope and Grump took over the hearth with their cooking.

Sleepy, fully dressed now, came over to Snow.

"You all right?"

Snow moved to sit up in the bed, the furs falling to his waist, exposing his pale chest. "I have to pee."

"It's fine. We have a water closet all the way in the back. Want me to carry you there?"

In truth, Snow had to do more than pee. He nodded. Then he said, voice scratchy, "How do you have a water closet?"

"We finished off a far back section of the cave with wood. There's a pit there. You know caves—it might be bottomless for all we know. It's very handy when we're snowed in and can't empty chamber pots or go outside for other business."

Snow nodded. "I'm sure."

He was used to water closets in the palace. But then the palace had every amenity. It was built and added onto through the ages to become the luxurious stronghold and ruling castle it was. There was even a well for water, and windmills that powered a system to bring water to the palace kitchens.

Sleepy came to Snow's side, pushing back the furs. He lifted him in his strong arms, as if Snow were a child.

Snow laughed shyly, reaching to cover his nakedness. "A blanket, please."

Sleepy said, "Why would someone as beautiful as you cover yourself? Ever?"

Doc shushed him, making a waving motion with his hand that distracted the cat from eating. She perked her ears up, watching them.

"Careful, Sleepy," Doc said. "Not everyone is like us. Or thinks as we do."

"Or has our predilections," Grump added, stirring something in a pot.

Just then, Bash came out from the back of the cave, frowning as he heard that last sentence. He lowered his head and hid behind his long, brown bangs. Snow could see his cheeks were aflame.

Sleepy grinned with that sweet, beautiful mouth. "Snow's fine. Aren't you, Snow?"

Snow said, "No, it's okay. I just—I'm not used to such openness. I think you all are wonderful. Just—wonderful." His sentence trailed off with a sigh.

"Well, now that Sleep has you up, maybe you can eat with us?" Doc asked. "How do your feet feel?"

"Throbbing, but I think maybe better." Snow really wasn't sure, but he wanted to let Doc know he appreciated everything he'd done for him.

"That's good," Doc said. "For goddess's sake. Get him a blanket, Bash."

Bash went into the other, darker part of the house, then quickly re-emerged with a fuzzy folded, soft cloth hemmed all the way around. "I made this," he said, calmly unfolding it and placing it over Snow.

Snow, still reclining in Sleepy's arms, looked down at it. It was soft pink wool, and perfectly hemmed. "It's beautiful," Snow said. "Thank you."

"All right," Sleepy said. "Let's take the tour."

Snow clutched at Sleepy's shoulder as the man effortlessly strode into the mysterious dark.

Snow looked all around, trying to make out what he could without much light. He blinked and saw six neat beds all on wood frames with lovely, full mattresses piled with pillows, blankets and furs. He wondered why the seventh bed was separate and more to the front. Had they moved it for him?

Each bed was paired with a bedside table, and the surfaces were littered with candles and candle ends, all unlit now.

At the foots of the beds were trunks, also made of wood, where the men could store belongings, and Snow could tell they'd been lovingly built. At least a dozen hooks lined one wall and on it were an array of robes, belts and shirts.

These men had worked hard to make their house a home.

"Not much light back here," Sleepy said, moving forward through the giant bedroom.

Snow heard dripping water but couldn't see where it came from.

Sleepy turned and used his body to part a curtain that led further back. The ceiling slanted downward. The openness of the cave narrowed. But now Snow could see the wooden privacy walls surrounding a neatly built, seatless chair over a hole in the ground. The water closet. The toilet.

In the darkness, Snow could still see that the walls were lined with herbs and dried flowers which kept the scent of the toilet at bay. Pretty *and* efficient. These men thought of everything.

Sleepy seemed not embarrassed at all as he set Snow down upon the seatless chair and arranged his blanket over his lap.

"I'll be right out here. Call when you're done. There are rags for, well, you know."

Snow nodded. "Thank you."

Sleepy gave him his warm smile again, and Snow felt it from his face to his toes. That smile. Sweet. Generous. And all for him.

When Snow finished, Sleepy came and picked him up again. He took him down the other side of the room apart from the beds where the wall of the cave curved to form almost another whole room. It was more an alcove, and the rocks there were wet and Snow heard more dripping sounds.

"Do you have a leak?"

"It's all good. We need the ventilation. But yes, it leaks here. Look." He pointed to some pots on the ground where the drips, flashing in errant light leaking from the front room, landed.

"We collect a lot of our washing water this way. When it's too cold to go out, or we're snowed in, we always have water. It's always dripping here. All the time. There are holes to the outside. It gives us air. There is a big tree to one side. It keeps even the deepest of snows from covering the all the vents. We won't suffocate."

"That's amazing," Snow said.

It was the perfect home. And for seven men to survive the long winters of the White Hills, it was efficient, warm, and cozy. And they all had each other. Snow could not think of a better place to be.

"All right," Sleepy said. "Do you feel well enough to sit with us at the table?"

"Yes. I do. But I have no clothes."

"We don't mind." Sleepy chuckled. "But all right. You can use one of my cloaks. I have two. I'll give you the red one. You can keep it. It will look so lovely on you with your coloring."

Snow blushed at the compliment. He felt he was nothing in comparison to these men with their physical beauty and enviable camaraderie.

Sleepy pretended not to see Snow's response. As he entered the main, front room with the hearth, he said, "Here. You can sit by me."

He lowered Snow into a chair and arranged his blanket for him, then stood and said, "I'll get that cloak."

He returned with a beautiful red cloak, wool-lined, hemmed with gold thread.

It reminded Snow of the purple robe his father had given him on his eighteenth birthday. Just before the king had died. He'd been wearing it the night of his almost-murder.

"I had a cloak when I arrived, I think," he said.

Doc turned as Snow spoke. "Nothing of your clothing could be saved, I'm afraid. I'm sorry."

"But—" Snow frowned. He didn't recall that it had been damaged. The huntsman had not managed to cut him or his clothing. But he didn't argue.

"I'm sorry," Doc repeated. "Did the cloak mean a lot to you?"

"It was a gift from my father. All I had left."

"I'm sorry," Doc said.

The other men exchanged guilty looks, but Snow said nothing. If they had destroyed his clothes, there had to be a good reason. But he couldn't help a tinge of grief at losing the last thing that defined his identity.

Hap seemed to sense the turn of mood. In a bright voice, he said, "The red cloak will be absolutely handsome on you. Sleepy never wears it anyway. He likes his brown one."

"Here," Sleepy said, standing behind Snow. "Let me help you put it on."

The cloak did not have sleeves, but it had holes cut in the sides for his arms to poke through. Snow let Sleepy drape it over him and arrange it all around him. He helped him get his arms through the holes.

Snow kept the blanket in his lap for extra warmth.

The porridge was served.

Hot and steaming, it smelled good. The men offered Snow butter and honey as well.

"Where do you get butter this time of year," Snow asked.

"A farm down the way." Doc spooned a big helping into his mouth. "They have dairy cows. We trade well with them. So don't you worry about eating too much."

The others all nodded their agreement as if they had already decided that everything that was theirs was Snow's as well.

Flustered by their trust and generosity, Snow could not respond. All he could do was focus on eating.

His stomach growled. He was so hungry.

Two helpings later, he realized for someone recovering from serious injuries, he had probably eaten too much. Lethargy and exhaustion reclaimed him.

Snow turned to Sleepy. "I don't think I can move, I ate so much."

"Don't worry. I'll take you back to bed." His pretty smile turned to a grin, as if he laughed away the suggestiveness of his words.

Chapter Eight

Every day was much like the last. Snow woke to Sleepy's arms around him, and that naked, muscular body pressed tight to him for warmth through the long winter's night.

The routine became normal to him, comforting.

He would listen as several of the six other men made love in the large, dark bedroom beyond the front room, with Snow flushing and imagining what they might be doing to each other. The only one who didn't join in was Sleepy. He stayed with Snow, always by his side.

Snow would watch as each man bathed before the firelight. He realized they were all healthy and handsome, and quite affectionate after whatever went on in the back bedroom, as they sometimes offered to wash each other's backs.

Sleepy would rise, bathe as Snow watched, and then take him to the back of the cave for his bodily functions.

They would eat breakfast. Then Sleepy would take a pail of warm water and sponge-bathe Snow.

Snow was shy at first, but he soon grew used to it, and looked forward to bath time. The warm water and Sleepy's hands were gentle. The big man did not presume any intimacy beyond the bath, or sleeping together at night. He respected Snow's space and privacy, and allowed Snow to clean his own body in the private areas.

Still, Snow's affection for Sleepy grew quickly. Every time Sleepy climbed into bed with him at night, Snow's heart began to pound and his skin would tingle.

Five days a week, the men would go away to work in the quarry, leaving Snow alone to read, nap and heal.

For the first few days, Snow spent most of his time sleeping. He battled on again/off again fevers.

Though the men's home was comfortable and warm when the hearth fire roared, and they left him plenty of food and water within reach so he would not have to get up and crawl to find it, he still grew lonely.

Sil often came to nap at the bottom corner of his bed. Since he'd passed her strict cat-approval process, she now purred herself to sleep. She kept him company and he was grateful.

The fifth day, Friday, he was happier because he knew the men would be home for two days. Now he could get to know them better. He would not be left alone for so long.

His excitement over the coming weekend—Doc had said maybe he could get out of bed at last and try to take some steps—kept him from sleeping. He had a couple books on loan from Bash, who loved to read as much as Snow did, a candle burning on the bed stand, and a ceramic mug beside a carafe of cold water. His lunch, some bread, dried meat, and salted cheese had long been eaten.

Everything was perfect. Almost silent. Calming.

For the first time in days, his feet did not ache so much.

The air was cool but warmer than usual, and not just from the hearth. He could hear the leaking water drips from the ceiling in the back room, melted ice falling with plunking noises from various crevices and leaks into lined up pots and pans.

Even though he had not been outside for days, Snow could sense it. The day had warmed. In his tower room, if he'd still been up there locked away, he would have felt the breezes change, and watch out his tiny window the sky go from white to dark blue.

Though winter really never left the White Hills, and summer lasted all but a couple months, the seasons could still be sensed and felt. Amid slow-to-melt snows, the trees still budded. Insects buzzed. Little wildflowers bloomed.

In the lowlands and the valleys, all still part of the White Hills realm, the farmers would be planting now, or at least planning their strategies. He could imagine the creeks running with whitewater, and all the precious animals bearing their young.

But up here on the mountain, the cold always remained, though not so bitter in summer, which was slowly approaching.

Snow leaned back, letting the book he'd been reading rest open on his chest.

He daydreamed happier times when his mother let him play in the winter garden where he built ice sculptures and pretended they were his friends. He loved the snow apples, cold with frost, and ate them plucked right off the sturdy orchard trees which bloomed late, and produced fruit on into December.

His mouth watered as he thought of apples. He hadn't had one in years. Nor apple pie, turnovers, tarts, or baked apples with cinnamon and raisins.

All he'd been fed in the prison tower room was simple food: hard rolls, potatoes, winter cabbage, chewy jerky, broth. All he'd had to drink was water.

He felt like a king here in the cave of the seven men. They cooked wonderful meals. They made sure he had enough until he was full. They were warm, generous and good-natured. Even Grump gifted him the occasional smile and friendly glance.

As Snow relaxed, he thought again of how close these men were with each other. How they bathed together, and even made love together. How listening to them love in the dark beyond the head of his bed made Snow feel both comforted and nervous at the same time. Nervous because he craved it, yet he'd never known anything like it for real. The old lady had been only cruel. Before that, he'd been a virgin.

Often, throughout the past days, Snow would replay all the images he'd saved in his mind of Sleepy bathing. Such elegance in strength, such an irresistible appeal. Sleepy's handsomeness fulfilled every detail of every fantasy Snow had had of other men in a sensual way.

What it came down to, when Snow made himself face the facts, was that he wanted the man. It was that simple and straight-forward.

Just thinking the thought make his face heat.

In his mind's eye he saw the gleaming bronze of his body, the curves and hollows of flexing muscles, the lovely dark shades of his hair curling at the ends against broad shoulders, the always ignored but sweetly bobbing cock with its so-pretty rosy tip. Every morning when Sleepy got up to bathe, his sleep erection begged for attention. Snow dared a shy thought of being the one to give that sort of attention to Sleepy.

Basking in that vision, Snow was startled from his pleasant reverie by a loud thump. Then another.

He pushed himself up in bed, balancing on his palms. Heart quickening.

More thumping commenced, this time three more loud thwacks.

The sound echoed down from the narrow hall that let up to the small wooden door in the earth. The door that led to his underground sanctuary. His refuge.

Snow's skin prickled in fear. A cold sweat broke out all over his body, itching at his back.

The cat lifted her head. Sniffed the air. Then got up and went under the big dinner table.

Snow heard some distant scrambling at the door, and some more loud thwacks.

He knew he should stay very quiet and still, but his instinct was to run. He couldn't walk, but he could maybe crawl. Find some place to hide.

He had the little wool blanket Bash had given him, and Sleepy's attractive red cloak lay draped across the foot of the bed.

Snow grabbed up both and slowly let his body slide from the bed. His chest tightened in the cool air, and his breaths caught with fear.

Neither Sleepy nor Doc had told him to expect any visitors. Ever.

He had the brief thought that maybe someone needed help. But then discarded it. He was being hunted. He could not allow himself to even consider going to the door and opening it.

Shivering at the notion that the huntsman might still be out there hunting him, looking to cut him apart with that gleaming knife of his, he decided the cat had the right plan. Hide.

On his hands and knees, he draped the red cloak about his naked shoulders. He took the small, pink wool blanket and wadded it under his arm. Then he crawled toward the back of the cave where the big bedroom was, and the other six beds. The trickling water splashing into various pots and pans grew louder.

The pounding on the door continued, more distant now, but still shocking. Even if whoever knocked was not the huntsman, it could be a stranger, or a group of strangers. They could be thieves. They could be the queen's guard.

Snow's body shuddered harder as he crawled toward to rearmost shadows, his sore feet dragging every time he lost his balance. A baby could crawl better than he right now.

Beside himself with fear and cold, Snow kept going until he reached the water closet. He saw the silhouettes of the herbs and dried flowers, smelled the spice of them and not the latrine itself. Dope liked to brag about how clean he kept the area, using sudsy water to wash the area down every day. "Seven men," he'd said, "could commit to live like pigs if we let things go too long without a thorough cleaning."

And now with Snow, there was an eighth man.

Dope had done a good job. The refuse scent was diminished, hardly noticeable. The herbs scented the air in a pleasant manner. This was also an area where Snow had learned the men could do a little laundry now and again as they needed it. But today there was no sign of the laundry buckets or piles of dirty clothes.

Snow moved on his hands and knees behind the far wooden privacy wall where the ceiling sloped down to the floor leaving only a few feet of space. Back against this far corner, a few dusty boxes were stored. The air was freezing. It wafted up from distant spaces too narrow to get through, sharp, cold. The underworld.

He wrapped his cloak tighter around himself, and squeezed between the rock wall and the wooden privacy wall, and bent his knees tight to his chest. He brought up the cloak's hood, then used the little wool blanket for extra protection against his feet which were now aching with renewed and extreme pain.

He wrapped the blanket about his feet and gave extra cushion beneath them, then huddled in the dark space and listened to the whining air vent up from the smaller passages.

Snow lay his head on his knees and shut his eyes. He listened.

The pounding on the front door did not return. What could that mean? Maybe the person—or persons—went away. Or maybe the door had opened.

Snow blinked, watching the shadows move in the front room. He knew they undulated because of the fire, but the darker side of his mind feared an intruder.

He hunkered down in his hood, drawing the red cloak close about his body. Images of the old lady and all her power as queen came unbidden to him. Maybe she found out he was alive. Maybe one of the men let it slip out at work that they had a foundling in their home.

Sudden images of the queen's abuse filled his mind. He cringed, trying not to remember her version of touch—slaps and shoves and all the indignities of her use of Snow in her bedchamber.

He could not go back to that. He *would* not. He would escape. Run until he died.

His body was shaking now. The cold came up from the rocky, earthen floor. Even with the wool blanket wrapped double around them, his feet grew cold. The ache felt as if the huntsman's knife had found its mark and was now chopping him into little bits to feed to the wolves, starting with his feet.

He heard nothing from the front room except perhaps little snaps and pops from the hearth fire. No footsteps. No voices. But still, he could not bring himself to crawl back to warmer spaces.

What if the old lady waited for him? With her cold hands and hateful words? With chains to bind him and take him back to the little tower room? Or worse, she could be waiting with a sword to cut out his heart, as she had already ordered.

Snow shivered uncontrollably, and his mind fell into darker thoughts until he lost track of time.

In the midst of his nightmare visions playing across his mind, he heard low moans and realized his breathing was stuttering because he was shaking so hard.

All of a sudden, he heard a loud bang. And this time there were footsteps.

His heart raced. He couldn't breathe. Everything spun.

And then he heard the voices. So familiar. Sounds he'd come to find comfort in. To love.

They began to call out.

"Snow, where are you?"

He recognized Doc and Hap and Sleepy. Then all of the others. He wanted to call out, but he had no voice. It was lost deep in his throat, frozen. He was ice and nothing more. The lost winter prince of the White Hills.

Footsteps came closer to the water closet and the space where Snow hid.

He heard Dope say, not two feet away, "Hey." Then, "I found him! He's by the water closet. He doesn't look so well."

More boot steps sounded, close, closer.

"Move! I've got him."

Thank the goddess, it was Sleepy. Warm arms came around him and pulled his head to a strong chest. He could smell Sleepy's unique scent. Even after working all day, he was all woodsy and old leaf, and pine with an autumn-ness about him Snow craved.

Sleepy was the tallest and strongest of the men, so it was nothing for him to pull Snow into a cradling embrace and lift him as Sleepy stood on steady legs.

"I've got you," came the soft voice in Snow's ear. "You're safe."

Snow lifted his head and opened his eyes. He tried to put his free arm around Sleepy's neck. But he was shivering so much his muscles weren't working. He could only press his hand, palm flat, against the muslin covering the curve of muscle beneath which Sleepy's kind heart beat.

Quickly, he was back in his bed again, the furs pulled aside, and Sleepy busying himself with getting the cloak out of the way.

Snow realized his face was wet. Embarrassed, he turned away. He didn't mean to push at Sleepy, but he felt so vulnerable.

"It's all right," Sleepy said.

Doc was on the other side of the bed. He placed a gentle hand on Snow's forehead. "Do you have a fever, son?" he asked.

He was weak. Cold and scared. He feared he'd never get past it. Never be able to walk free, live a normal life, let alone be the prince again.

"What happened?"

Snow sensed the other men, still and silent as they watched and listened, curious. Caring.

He still couldn't find his voice.

"He isn't hot," Doc said. He went to the foot of the bed and pushed the furs back to assess his feet. "Dressings need to be changed."

Snow felt Doc begin to unwrap them. They ached so.

Sleepy folded the red cloak and pulled the furs tight about Snow's now naked body. He sat on the edge of the bed facing Snow, and leaned down, putting his hands behind Snow's neck and pulling him up into a sort of hug. He supported all of Snow's upper body weight with his arms.

"You're cold from sitting back there in the depths of his place," Sleepy said. "Why were you back there?"

A voice that sounded like Hap said, "Maybe something scared him."

Snow nodded against Sleepy's shoulder.

"Well, what was it?"

"Probably a mouse or something," Grump offered from across the room.

"Quiet! It's not that," Sleepy argued.

Doc said quietly, "His feet are swollen again. Cold. Let's get him closer to the fire."

"I'm going to lift you up again," Sleepy told Snow.

Snow rubbed his face on Sleepy's tunic and nodded. He was so grateful for the man. For all of them. They would never harm him. He knew that. He had nothing to fear now.

He opened his mouth to speak, but still his voice was lost.

"He's still startled," Sleepy said, lifting Snow who was now naked. "Let's get him warm and something to eat. Then he'll talk."

Snow felt Sleepy's chin rub the top of his bowed head.

Someone came with blankets and piled them on top of him. Another brought cushions. Someone else stirred up the fire in the hearth. Another man brought Snow a cup of hot coffee. Bitter.

Slowly, Snow came to his senses. He heard the familiar banging around of men preparing food. Others were taking off their boots, or moving into the other parts of the home to change their shirts, do laundry, or visit the water closet.

Snow sat on the cushions with the blankets wrapped around him before the hearth. He drank the hot coffee and felt it go all the way down, warming him.

Sleepy sat beside him, cross legged, free hand in his lap. He had a cup of coffee in his other hand which he sipped. The steam curled up into his face.

"Better?" Sleepy asked.

Snow nodded. He cleared his throat. "Someone was here."

All the men stopped what they were doing and turned toward him. Grump and Dope came from the sleeping area.

"What?" Doc came forward, standing over him.

"They pounded on the door for a long time."

Sleepy put his hand on Snow's leg. "So you hid."

Snow nodded.

Doc said, "Could be Hans from the farm."

"Could be," Hap said, tilting his head.

"But he knew we were working," Grump added.

Doc shot him a dark look. Snow knew it was for his benefit. They didn't want him to be scared.

"Since my death is unproven, the people who wanted to kill me are probably looking for me," Snow said. His voice shook, gravelly. He focused on breathing in, out.

"You are safe as long as you're with us," Doc said. "And here, you are secure. As long as you never venture out alone."

"What if they come back?" Snow shifted in his blankets. Some of the coffee sloshed onto his hand, but it wasn't hot enough to burn.

"You are never to answer the door alone. If we're here, one of us will, but you will stay back," Doc said.

Snow nodded. "But if it's the queen's guard—" He stopped, not wanting to say too much.

"We haven't seen them around too much," Sleepy assured him.

"But no one could keep them from forcing themselves in," Grump supplied.

"They won't," Sleepy said, never taking his eyes off Snow.

Snow enjoyed Sleepy's comfort, but soft words did not change the truth. If the queen's guard wanted something, they would get it. If the old lady commanded her men at arms, they asked no questions. They blindly obeyed.

Bash came forward, then. "More coffee?" he asked sweetly, holding out the pot.

Both Snow and Sleepy held out their cups. This time, Bash offered them a bowl of sugar to sweeten its bitter taste.

Bash said, "It was probably Hans. He wanted to trade and thought maybe one of us stayed home today. He knows it's not a rare week when one of us stays home for a day to keep the house."

Hap nodded. "Bash is right. Today's Friday. We don't work tomorrow. I'll go down to his farm and ask him. We could use some milk and eggs anyway." He grinned. "Maybe he'll have made some of his famous winter apple pies. One can hope."

Snow's mouth watered at the thought. He missed pie, and apple pies the most. In fact, he'd just been thinking about apples this very day.

He tried to imagine the farm, with dairy cows and perhaps orchards leaning into a hill. The house might be white with red eaves and windows glowing gold from within. Cozy, warm. Full of food and cats. And maybe children who played catch-the-wren all winter and sledded down the steepest slopes.

He had been cooped up for too long. Not only in this lovely cave-made-home, but in the tower as well.

The scent of miner's stew filled the front room. Venison, gravy, carrots, potatoes. Thick, salted and peppered, it would be served with fresh bread and butter.

Snow's stomach rumbled. He shifted his feet, which were bare right now. Doc hadn't re-wrapped them.

Snow pulled the blankets up and looked down at them for the first time since he'd been rescued. They were pink and peeling, but not as swollen as they felt. He was surprised to see two pink nubs where the tips of his little toes had been. They didn't look too terrible. They'd been stitched. He had not remembered or known about that. It had all happened while he'd been unconscious. Luckily.

Though getting better, his feet were far from normal. He had a lot of healing to do.

"Feet hurt?" Sleepy asked.

Snow gave him a half smile. He had caused them enough drama for the evening. He did not wish to complain more. Their constant ache, like a fever or a headache but in his feet, never receded. They got worse when he banged them on something like the edge of the bed, or the floor when crawling to hide from thieves.

Walking. He could barely imagine it. It would be like toddling onto pins and needles, all face up. But Doc had said he might be ready to take some steps this weekend. He would try not to disappoint him.

When Sneezy started dishing up the stew, Sleepy said, "Think you might like to join us at the table."

Snow nodded.

"Good."

"Can you get my cloak," Snow asked.

Sleepy winked. "I love your modesty." He stood and went to retrieve it.

After Sleepy helped Snow into the cloak, fastening it for him at the throat, helping him put his arms through the holes in the sides, he lifted Snow into his arms, standing without a moment's loss of balance.

He brought Snow to the chair he'd sat in before, and sat beside him.

Still rattled, Snow was at least able to eat. Two helpings of stew and two thick slices of bread.

After dinner, Sneezy and Dope moved off to a smaller round table and played checkers.

Feeling overly full, Snow watched as Bash and Hap and Grump brought out a deck of cards. The cards were lovely, with stamped scenes of horses and farms on the backs.

Bash said, shuffling the deck, "Join us?" He looked directly at Snow.

Sleepy said, "I will."

"Okay, but how do you play?" Snow asked.

"You've never played cards before?"

Snow knew the guards played cards, but he'd never learned. No one had taken any time to teach him.

"Hearts, I say," Hap said.

"We'll teach you," Sleepy said.

"It's fun," Bash added.

"Unless you get the queen of spades," said Grump. "We call her Serena."

"Grump," Doc said, shaking his head.

"But not tonight. Tonight we won't call her anything." Grump frowned, bowing his head.

"What to join us, Doc?" Sleepy asked.

"Well, not if you want me to finish knitting that pair of socks you need." Doc took up a basket filled with skeins of wool, and round, colorful balls of yarn. He sat by the fire, pulled out a pipe, and lit it. Then he started searching the contents of the basket.

Sil came up to him and tried to get in his lap, but there was no room. Instead, she settled on the round, woven rug by the fire.

Snow had his first game of Hearts. It wasn't difficult. He learned quickly. He won the first time around, but suspected the others had gone easy on him to let him learn. He decided it was the most fun he'd had, in, well, ever. He even found himself laughing with the others as they played their hands.

Every time Snow laughed, Sleepy would look aside at him, his brown eyes sparkling.

After a while, Sleepy said, "I have not ever heard you laugh. It's nice."

Grump rolled his eyes.

Bash's eyebrows went straight up to mid-forehead.

Hap elbowed Sleepy. "Sweet on him?" he whispered.

Snow, feeling his face heat, said, "I don't really remember the last time I laughed."

Hap said, "That's terrible. Like a condition. A bad one."

"Hell, Hap, not everyone needs to laugh or be happy all the time to be healthy," Grump argued.

Snow laughed again to see the ease with which they bantered.

More cards were dealt. The night deepened. The game went on.

Chapter Nine

In one way, Snow became used to sleeping with Sleepy. They had a built-in chemistry. They got along. Snow relied on Sleepy to carry him, to bathe him, to help him in every way.

But in another way, he could not get used to a naked body all warm and cozy up against him night after night and, now that he was feeling somewhat better, fail to have a response. A physical response.

Though Sleepy rose every morning sporting an enticingly beautiful erection which he never commented about, yet showed no shyness in revealing, Snow was mortified at the thought that he might be caught sporting his own.

He thought his unease probably came from the way he'd been treated by the old lady. He still had nightmares. He never stopped worrying that the huntsman and the queen's guard would always be searching for him until the end of days.

Snow would eventually have to leave the kingdom to have an ordinary life some day.

Saturday morning came and those who wanted to catch some extra rest after a hard week slept in.

Snow, however, woke early when the only movement in the front room was the cat bathing herself before the orange hearth embers. The ash had piled up and looked like soft gray waves in a little sunset sea.

Sil's big green eyes fixed on Snow, and for half a minute they stared at each other. He smiled, thinking she was quite a fine creature and wondered if she ever got to go outside and see the sun. The woods would be a dangerous place for such a small, tame animal. But every living thing needed light.

Snow was tired of being abed, even if he did have a big handsome guy to keep him warm. He longed to see the sun again. His body ached from being immobile. He wondered if today might be the day he could take a few steps past the wooden front door. He wouldn't go far. And he was sure Sleepy, if not a few of the others, would accompany him.

After a good night's sleep, he'd mostly gotten over the scary thumps he'd heard. He was still afraid, but surely a few minutes in the sun and then quickly back inside would do no harm.

His heart raced at the thought.

The cat jumped up on the big table and started to sniff about, her fur a beautiful silvery gray in the firelight.

Sleepy shifted behind Snow, his body warm and strong. They barely touched. Sleepy's knees brushed gently against the backs of Snow's own. His hands were crossed and the forearms arms touched against Snow's upper back. His breath, which had been rumbling slightly in sleep, quieted, the air brushing the nape of Snow's neck.

From one moment to the next, Snow could tell that Sleepy had wakened. He knew his sleep habits, the sounds he made, the way his body felt relaxed against him, and when he was just being still while awake.

Snow turned a little so that his shoulder brushed Sleepy's chin.

"Morning," Sleepy whispered.

"Hi."

"How are you feeling?"

"All right, I think."

"Your feet?"

"Quite ugly, I think, after seeing them for the first time last night."

Their whispers came soft, the sound feathering the air about them, their breaths warm against the blankets and furs. It was intimate and cozy. Wonderful.

"They aren't ugly, nor is the rest of you."

Snow pressed his lips tightly together upon hearing the compliment. "Thank you." His whisper was so soft he thought Sleepy might not have heard it.

"They'll heal all right," Sleepy added.

"Well, you're not, either," Snow boldly stated.

"What?"

"Ugly, I mean."

"Oh." Sleepy let out a long sigh. "That's very nice."

In the cover of near-darkness, Snow felt secure enough to make a confession. "Well, you're very nice to look at. But you probably know that."

"Am I? I don't mind you looking."

Snow let out a soft snort, suppressing a laugh.

"I want you to know I will never do you harm. I'll never do anything to make you uncomfortable."

"I know that."

"I promise," Sleepy said.

"You don't have to promise. You've taken good care of me. We've been in the same bed for nearly a week and you've been a complete gentleman."

It was true. Even when they heard the sounds of lovemaking every morning from the other part of the cave, Sleepy had never presumed a thing. Though it was a revelatory shock when Snow had realized some of the men in the household were lovers, and that they paraded around naked in front of each other, none of them had made any uncomfortable advances toward him.

Their nudity was a natural part of their day. And why shouldn't they be unclothed in their very own home? And love each other in all ways if they wished? It was quite terrific, actually.

These men. Snow wished with all his heart they were his real family. Like brothers. The brothers he, as an only child, had always wanted.

"Sleepy, how long have you all been living here?" Snow asked.

"Some of us… ten years. Dope's been with us two. Bash for five."

"And you?"

"Six years. When I met Doc at the quarry, I didn't have a home."

Snow wanted to ask why, but didn't want to pry. He'd already gathered that the men here had sad or dark pasts. They went by nicknames, which meant they didn't want anyone to know who they had been.

"I know you want to know more," Sleepy whispered. "And you will. In time. But of course you must know that ever since the second queen came to be in the Palace of the White Hills, that things changed. Times got hard for everyone in this realm. Obviously, times have been rough for you, too."

Snow nodded, biting down on his lower lip. But he hadn't known. Not the extent to which Sleepy now insinuated. He did not realize until coming here that the entire surrounding lands had suffered some sort of hardship. Like a blight. Indeed, the queen did rule with a hard hand, and while Snow's father had been alive she'd heavily influenced him. Snow had seen him whither and age before his eyes under the weight of the queen's demands. Things had been getting bad for years before Snow's father finally died.

Snow had not thought the heaviness and gloom in the palace had extended to the surrounding lands and townships. He'd been too young. He'd not thought that far ahead of himself and his tiny world.

"But I didn't know all of what you just said now," Snow said. His lungs heaved. "I've been imprisoned." Had he said too much?

"So. You were in prison?"

Snow nodded. And the terror slowly began to overtake him again, like the cold hand of a giant closing around him never to let go. If he told all of his story to Sleepy and the others, these men might be put in danger. Or put themselves in danger protecting him, or enact some sort of revenge.

His mouth was dry when he finally answered. "Like you all, I had bad times. But sheltered from the world. Kept away from it."

"I'm sorry," Sleepy said. He put his arm under Snow's pillow and pulled him closer so that his shoulder butted Sleepy's chest.

"Me, too. I'm sorry for all of you having hard times, too," Snow replied.

For a while, they lay together in their own little envelope of heat, staring up at the rocky roof. Snow could see tiny flashes of white light, like snowflake crystals embedded in the cave-stone. Indoor stars. They'd comforted him when he'd been in the most fevered pain the first couple of days after his rescue. He'd stare at them pretending they were wishing stars, hoping for reprieve from his continual pain and fear.

In the distant back of the cave, he could hear the constant drip-drip of the water from the vents splashing into the pots. Someone coughed. Men shifted in their beds. Whispering began, and shushing sounds of cloth.

It was so peaceful and Snow never wanted the moment to end.

The soft sounds of lovemaking from the other room came to him. Sighs and gasps. Nothing more.

Many mornings were like this, and Snow found it less embarrassing with every day, and more and more lovely and comforting. At first he'd thought it was only three of the men. Hap and Dope and Sneezy. But after some time, he saw an affection between them all, and realized they might take different partners each morning. Even Doc, who once was late to emerge from the back, showed signs of having joined in once in a while in the early morning observances to pleasure. But there also appeared to be couples. He thought maybe Doc and Bash were more to each other. Also, Sneezy and Grump.

Sleepy lay with his hip and shoulder now pressed to Snow's back and side. Their flanks lightly touched.

Snow did not dare turn toward him even an inch more. He had an erection and was already embarrassed that he couldn't control it. Even though the men behaved freely with their bodies here, and no one judged anyone else aside from a few joking remarks, Snow still felt constrained. Contained as if from a prison within he'd yet to fully escape.

The erection came from listening to the men make love, but also from his contentment at being here, away from the old lady and all the bad things in the palace. But mostly it came from the nearness of Sleepy who was too lovely to ignore.

He liked the closeness, and Sleepy, but hid it because he wasn't ready. He hid it from Sleepy because he worried if Sleepy found out and thought he was uncomfortable, Sleepy might stop spending the night with him, and take up space in one of the other men's beds until another bed could be obtained.

There had been so much poison in his life. Now all Snow wanted was hearth tales and warm porridge, a local farmer's winter apple pie and beautiful Sleepy at his side. Sil the cat. Games of Hearts. Doc's spectacles glowing orange with the fires of home. And this. The warmth of early mornings. The sounds of quiet love.

So many treasures he'd found here in such a short time. Generosity. Warmth of soul. A temporary stone paradise. Constellations in the ceiling.

And Sleepy, oh Sleepy. Snow's chest went all shaky and burned from within at the thought of Sleepy, his beauty, and somehow through all of Snow's bleak and abused existence, he wanted this man.

What was happening to him?

An old children's story of a foundling boy came unbidden to his mind. How the boy suffered as an orphan and then as a slave, but a good soul helped him and the boy found love and his happily ever after. He'd loved that story as a child, even if it had darkness within before the boy found his heart.

Snow shifted on the ticking of the bed mattress, and Sleepy shifted, too, his soft curls tumbling against Snow's cheek.

In this moment, Snow wondered if this was his own story, similar to his childhood favorite, about finding his own heart. For he could not imagine ever wanting anything more than this man beside him, touching him, keeping him safe.

Chapter Ten

Doc treated Snow's feet with hemp oil that stunk, but helped ease the pain. He wrapped them carefully, put him in a pair of thick wooly socks, and loaned him a pair of Sneezy's boots.

Sneezy had the biggest feet of all the men, and his boots would be roomy for the combined wrappings and thick stocks.

Hap loaned Snow a white muslin shirt.

Dope gave him a pair of trousers since they both seemed to be the same size, slim-hipped and lean, and not quite as tall as the rest.

With Sleepy's red cloak, Snow was ready for his first trip outside.

Snow sat on the bed, his legs dangling over the edge, feet flat but without weight on the stone cave floor.

"Wait!" Doc held up his hand. "We forgot one thing!"

Sleepy and Snow looked up.

"What?" Snow asked.

Doc ran to his knitting basket, then came back with a dark lump in his hand. He held it out.

It was a black knit cap.

"This was what I was making last night."

Slowly, Snow reached out to take the gift. "I—I—don't know what to say. It's—it's beautiful!"

Doc took it from him, shrugging, and stretched it over Snow's head. "Your blond hair is a dead giveaway if anyone sees you. Not that anyone really ventures this far up in the hills. But that knocking on the door concerns me. So we'll keep your pale hair a secret for now."

Doc pulled the cap over Snow's ears and gently tucked his hair under the edges until he was completely covered.

"There. Now you're ready."

Sleepy directed a handsome grin at Snow. "You look set for anything."

Snow began to lift himself up at the same time Doc and Sleepy got on either side of him and helped him to stand.

He wobbled for a moment. The soles of his feet throbbed as if pierced, stabbed. The ache gave him the notion his feet would shatter like glass if he took a step. But it was an illusion of fear and prickly pain combined.

"How does it feel?" Doc asked.

"Like knives. I can deal with it, but I'm afraid I'll stumble."

"We'll take it slow," Doc said.

"I won't leave your side," Sleepy added.

Together, they moved forward, and Snow took his first step.

He grabbed the arms of both men, using their support, but he realized he *could* walk. It hurt, but he was up.

A few more steps and the pain lessened a bit, and Snow got quickly better at dealing with his balance.

They all moved toward the passage to the outer door.

Going up the rocky incline was hard because there wasn't room for both Doc and Sleepy to remain at his side. Doc moved behind him. Sleepy was in front.

"Hang onto my shoulders for support," Sleepy instructed.

Snow did, going forward.

When Sleepy opened the round, wooden door, bright light rushed at Snow's eyes. He blinked back the sting and forged ahead.

Even knowing Hap and Sneezy and Bash had gone ahead to scout the area and make sure they were truly alone, Snow hesitated that last, painful step onto the ground outside the cave.

But he finally moved forward, and stood free. Sleepy and Doc stepped away and let him stand by himself.

He squinted until he got used to the newness of the light, then gazed about.

The view was breathtaking.

The air was crisp and cold, even in the ivory sunlight. Silver mountains rose up beyond a line of green pine. They were at a higher elevation than the White Hills palace.

Snow had seen this area in the dead of night, and in a stupor, so actually this was his first time looking at the forest where the men lived, and through which they walked to work every day.

There was white fluff on the air and at first Snow thought it was snowing. But these weren't icy flakes. Despite patches of white frost still on the ground, and thicker drifts under the trees, it was already May and the cottonwoods were blooming.

Snow put his head back and stared up at the wide, blue sky.

He'd had a view from his tower room for two years, but it faced south toward the valleys. It was in itself also spectacular, but narrow due to the thick stone walls. The bars on the window prevented him from sticking his head out to see anything but a slice of land and sky.

Other than the night he was almost killed, Snow had not been outside in two years.

He breathed in and smiled.

Doc nodded at him, his face younger in the morning light, less pale. He was a handsome man toughened only from working outdoors.

When Snow turned to look at Sleepy, his breath caught. Capless, Sleepy's hair reflected the light with a smooth shine like a mirror. Deep mahogany, it softened Sleepy's strong features, and there was a crown of light about his head that gave him a kingly look.

The whites of Sleepy's eyes glinted in the sunrays. An edge of wildness remained there, tamed to sweetness.

Something in Snow's chest lurched. His body tingled. He wanted him, yet they barely knew each other. Sharing a bed bonded them, but Snow did not know Sleepy's past, or his mind and heart. Not really.

"I forgot." Snow's voice came low in his throat.

"Forgot what?" Sleepy asked.

"How beautiful. How big. The world."

"You've missed this for more than a week, then."

Snow nodded. "As I said this morning. I was kept locked away. For a long time."

"And now you're with us," Doc said. "You don't have to say more unless you want to. None of us will pry."

"It's best if I remain a stranger for now. If you knew more, I would be afraid for you."

Sleepy and Doc exchanged glances which hinted to Snow that they knew more than they said. But Snow knew they would remain silent on the matter until Snow was ready to talk.

Could he ever reveal to them that he was a prince? *The* Prince of the White Hills?

He wasn't sure, but either way, he knew the men would never pressure him.

In the high altitude, the chill never quite went away, but it was May and spring. Birds flitted about in the trees which wore new green leaves. Grass sprouted around their trunks and along a narrow path that led into more trees.

Snow moved toward a copse of purple flowers by the entryway. "Rosemary?"

"Yes." Doc nodded.

Snow bent down and picked a sprig, waving it under his nose. It smelled pungent and sweet.

"Would you like to try a few more steps?" Sleepy asked.

"Yes."

Snow clung to Sleepy's arm with one hand, and clutched his purple rosemary bud in the other. He walked a large circle toward the edge of the trees where the pathway disappeared.

He looked back toward the little house in the hill, the cave of his healing. A red brick chimney rose from the ground where there were no trees, and gray smoke weaved through the blue air. That chimney and the wood door were the only clues that a home lay under the earth. Toward the other side of the hill, a tree bent, gnarled and old, over the ground. Snowdrifts lay about it.

That was where the leaking melt came from inside the cave that filled the men's pails and pots with water.

The environment exuded peace and harmony, everything at one with the earth and sky and air.

He heard chirping, buzzing, and low hums. Everything was alive here, working, whistling, in harmony with itself.

"Few know of this place," Doc said as Snow stared at the little hill. "You need not worry. Hap, Bash and Sneezy went to the farm two miles out, the one we talked about, to ask if Hans had come by. I'm sure they'll come back with a story that he was the one who'd visited and scared you half to death yesterday."

Snow sighed. "I hope so. I feel so stupid, but I couldn't stop thinking dark thoughts."

Snow walked a few steps in a circle.

"Your balance is getting better by the minute," Doc said. "We can work on herb tea and hemp ointment for the pain."

Snow felt the sun on his face like a caress. He tipped his head back again. "Thank you both. I can never repay you."

"We don't do this for pay," Sleepy said.

"The seven of us, after all we've been through, have a pact," Doc said. "Given a choice of two or more paths, we ask ourselves which one leads to the best, most right way to live. Saving you that night was not a difficult decision to make. It was the right thing to do."

"Were you the first to come here, Doc?" Snow asked.

He nodded. "I brought Bash with me. We discovered this cave and began to work on it to make it a home right away. We made the door, carved out the hearth and built the chimney. Over time, we hauled things up here on sleds. Beds. Tables. Dishes. And we also made some of it from the surrounding timber. Then Hap came along."

Taking up the story, Sleepy said, "Then Grump and Sneezy together. Then me. Dope was the last one to join us. It's been ten years for Doc. Six for me. Living here."

"You turned a hard life into a good life." Snow stated it almost as a question.

Both Sleepy and Doc nodded.

"Indeed, we did," Doc said.

Snow could not help but do the math. The years matched when his own misery started at the age of ten and the old lady came to live at the Palace of the White Hills.

It was as if she'd brought a malevolence with her into the realm and infested the surrounding lands with it. Snow had not been the only one affected, and obviously things only got worse as his father gave in to the queen and her opinions and demands.

If he had been older when it all happened, he might have been able to fight for the throne, and fight the old lady's tight grip on power. He might have been able to make things better. But he had been only ten, and helpless.

And now? He had nothing. No money. No power. No army to fight with.

But today was a good day. He was breathing. Walking. And the air was sweet. Everything was new, green amidst melting snow, fresh and alive. There might still be a few bars on his cage, but they were only in his mind.

As if Snow's thought had beckoned them forward, Hap, Sneezy and Grump came up the path from the woods, rucksacks draped over their shoulders. Their boots crunched dirt and leftover ice. They had proud smiles on their handsome faces.

Hap hurried toward Snow. "You're out! You're walking." He clapped him on the shoulder. "Good for you!"

The others came up alongside Hap.

Sneezy coughed once, but he was smiling wide. "You've got some color back in your face."

Grump said, with his usual wry look, but accompanied by a crooked half-smile, "Good for you."

Snow smiled shyly, shutting his eyes half-way. "Thank you. It does feel great to get out finally."

"It's a perfect day for it," Hap said.

Hap turned to Doc. "We came with news. Good news." He swung his sack to his side and looked down. "As well as three jugs of milk, cream, and a wooden box of eggs. Oh, and three fresh winter apple pies!"

Doc smiled, taking the heavy sack from Hap.

The other two set their sacks on the ground. "And we got other supplies, too," Grump said.

"Well, what's your news?" Doc asked.

"Snow will want to hear it, too."

Sleepy took a step closer to Snow, as if guarding him from anything from the outside world, even good news.

"It was indeed Hans who came by yesterday, thumping on the door. He said he thought Dope might be in, since he sometimes stays homes on Fridays to keep house. So all mysteries are solved."

Snow breathed in deep and let the air out in slow relief.

"What did Hans want?" Doc asked.

"Well, that he'd saved some pies for us, of course. He said he would have brought the supplies he put aside for us, but you know, he's sixty now. It's hard for him to carry anything up this hill, and right now his horse is lame. So he wanted Dope or Doc or whoever stayed home to come and get them. But no one answered. He left, figuring we might be by the farm today anyway."

"But what did you tell him? Not that we have guest. Please don't say you told him that!" Doc exclaimed.

"No. Of course not," Grump said. "We're not stupid. I said we saw footprints leading to the door in the mud and ice. We had wondered. That's all."

"Good. Snow is our secret for now. I hope all of you understand that."

The men nodded.

"Of course we do," said Sneezy.

Sleepy came closer to Snow, his elbow touching the side of Snow's arm. "No one can know," he said. "No one!"

Hap looked up at him. "Cool it, Sleep. We understand."

Snow turned his head aside and looked up at Sleepy. The man's eyes were narrowed, the facial muscles tight. The hollows of his cheeks had darkened, and his jaw formed a firm, tight line. He'd never seen him look so predatory, and protective.

Snow said, "I appreciate everything you are doing for me." He turned his gaze to Doc, Hap, Sneezy and Grump. "All of you."

"We won't allow harm to come to you," Doc said. "That's our promise."

"All I can say is I'm very lucky you all came along when you did. Or it would be my bones you'd be finding scattered in the woods."

Doc came up to him and touched him gently on the shoulder. "Well, some day you'll tell us the whole story, won't you." It wasn't a question.

Snow felt his throat tighten, but he nodded rapidly.

"But for now, let's take all these wonderful supplies indoors. We'll have a feast tonight by the heft and weight of these sacks."

"Hell, yeah," Hap said.

Sneezy chuckled. "I'm hungry already. That's quite a hike to and from Hans' farm." His brown hair, damp with sweat, hung in his eyes.

Grump's lighter brunet hair curved about his ears with sweat.

Hap's skin glowed in deepest brown from the sun and exertion.

Snow was not quite ready to go inside. He stiffened, not wanting to leave, his muscles craving more stimulation. He wished he could run and feel the breeze in his hair and on his face. He wanted to swing his arms over his head and spin like he used to when he was very young and his mother let him play in the kitchen's winter garden.

He wanted to pick flowers, talk to the bees, and feed bread crumbs to all the sparrows he could hear flitting about the thick trees.

The more he moved around, the less he felt the pain in his feet, and the better his balance. He didn't need help walking anymore. Distractions were wonders to the body.

Snow pushed his cloak back from his arms and body, the hood fallen aside, his loaned clothes on display, a little baggy but clean and warm, great gifts.

He was on the thin side, but these men would have him fed and filled out in no time. He was sure.

The sunlight beamed. His blood thrummed in his veins. He could taste the crisp sweetness of spring and didn't want to let his treat go.

Doc said, "You look like you'd like to stay out for a little longer."

"Well, if you all have work…" Snow did not want to be a burden to any of them.

Sleepy said, "I'll say with him." He crossed his arms over his broad chest.

"That should be fine," Doc said.

Snow looked up at Sleepy. "I'm grateful."

Sleepy showed him his white teeth. Then he let his arms down and bowed gracefully before Snow, his hair glimmering in the white light. "You deserve whatever you wish, my master," he said, chuckling.

Snow was floored. Sleepy had bowed for him.

Could these men know more than they were saying about who he was?

But it seemed less than possible. When Snow had turned eighteen and Serena had imprisoned him, word had immediately spread that the prince was dead. Only her closest, most loyal guards knew otherwise.

No one knew Snow had lived. But at times, it seemed to him that his seven saviors might have guessed he was more than another man with a tragic past.

Sleepy had to be just playing with him.

Snow said, "Don't do that." Then he laughed and backed up a little. He moved toward the path, awkward, but getting his footing better with each step. "I'm no one that important."

Sleepy answered his laugh. "You are important to me."

The others had all gone inside. The round wooden door stood open, and Snow heard the laughter and clatter of life indoors, the men enjoying themselves on a lovely spring day. The happy camaraderie of friends. Of family.

Light rays danced along hedges and the tops of trees. The mountain in the other direction held an inner purple shadow. Sky stretched overhead in a blue so abrupt, it nearly blinded.

Smoke from the brick chimney of the underground house silvered the air.

Snow laughed again and moved faster toward the copse of trees, and off the path a little where sprigs of grass were coming through the muddy topsoil. He almost tripped, then righted himself.

Sleepy followed him, keeping his pace slow, letting Snow get ahead of him.

A wind came up, shushing through the forest branches.

"I love it here!" Snow called to Sleepy.

The bigger man grinned. "Me, too."

Snow toddled off in another direction, Sleepy close behind.

Snow gave a little leap. Sleepy pretended to chase him. They played for a few minutes, both grinning, until Sleepy caught him up in his big arms.

"Gotcha," Sleepy shouted.

Snow gave a little yelp, but Sleepy's arms stayed tight around him. The man lifted him about an inch off the ground, grunting once. Then he touched his cheek to Snow's forehead, holding it there for a few seconds of breathless intrigue.

Suddenly, Sleepy let go. "Sorry." He looked sheepish.

Snow said, "For what? Why'd you let me go? If you catch me you have to keep me!"

He ran on, up a little incline.

Sleepy circled him like a playful predator.

But Snow grew tired very quickly.

His feet slid back and forth in the boots. Even with his thick socks and wraps, the boots were still a bit big for him. It soon became more painful to walk, and he'd strayed further from the door than he probably should have.

Breathing harder now, Snow tilted his head back to the white sun. For a second, it blinded him, and he closed his eyes seeing a rainbow of twirling colors behind his lids.

He faced the woods, knowing Sleepy had let him escape but was now slowly advancing, and opened his eyes, blinking away the afterimages of the bright light.

And there, far off, in a little clearing amid a copse of trees he saw a figure, a silhouette only. Definitely not a deer or wolf or any other animal. Tall. Two arms. Two legs. This was a human. And it was facing him. Watching.

"Sleepy!"

"What?" His guardian was approaching just a few yards off.

Snow motioned to him frantically. "Come here," he rasped.

Sleepy ran over to him, but as Snow blinked, the figure vanished, as if it had never really been there.

"I saw someone!"

"What?" Now Sleepy stood by Snow's shoulder, gazing in the direction where Snow looked.

"Or at least I thought I saw someone. A figure. Way off in those trees where you can see the white ground. It would swear I saw it."

"That's pretty far."

"But it was looking this way. Right at me."

Sleepy's hand touched Snow's upper arm. "Could you see details?"

"No. It was so far, but I would swear there was a person."

"Hap and Grunt and Sneezy checked these woods for signs of people. They found nothing. It was probably a deer. But I'll tell them to check again."

Snow gripped Sleepy's wrist where his hand touched him. "I could've imagined it. I was sun-blinded for a second. And it was so far. If I couldn't see details of him, then he couldn't really see me, either."

But Snow was so fearful the old lady might find him. Or that the huntsman was still hunting him, since no one knew if he was alive or dead. The men had subdued the queen's assassin, but they weren't sure if they had killed him.

"We should go back inside," Sleepy suggested. "I'm sorry; I know you want to stay out."

"I'm tired anyway." Snow shivered. A brittle breeze came up and shuffled through some wild lavender struggling along the tree line. The lacy shawl of a cloud flapped over the sun.

The land darkened.

The round open door of the seven men's home stood small and alone, far away enough that Snow had not realized the distance he had hobbled, mind numb with spring pleasure.

Sleepy offered his arm. Grateful, Snow took it, but every step back was a knife through the soles of each foot.

He stepped gingerly, but the boots made everything more awkward.

"I could carry ya'," Sleepy offered.

Snow's face heated. Embarrassed to be so needy. Embarrassed to want the physical contact. Too shy to agree, he said, "We're almost there."

He shivered a little more, trying to hide his discomfort. His pain. His fear.

If someone was watching him, he had no clue what he would do. He would never, ever want to put his new friends in danger.

If they were in danger from harboring Snow, Snow would have to leave. It broke his heart to even think it, but he would do what he had to do to protect his newfound friends.

Chapter Eleven

Sneezy and Hap came down the narrow, earthen passage and appeared, flustered and red-cheeked, in the front room.

"A storm's brewing," Hap declared.

"We looked everywhere you said and found no footprints, no signs of humans in the woods." Sneezy coughed, and hung his cloak on a hook by the door. He moved to take a cup of hot tea offered by Dope.

Sleepy ruffed up his own hair as he ran his hands through it in frustration. He sat with his elbows on the big wood table next to Snow. "Did you check where I told you out by the lightning tree near Leafbrook Creek?"

Hap came up behind Sleepy and put his hands on his shoulders. "Of course we did." He still wore his cloak. He leaned down and kissed Sleepy, a quick peck, on the top of the head. "We heard and obeyed you, dumb ass." The insult was used in a joking manner.

Undeterred, Sleepy said, "And all around Cutter's Ruin, too?"

"All around," Hap assured him. "There was a lot more snow still up there and there weren't even any footprints of wildlife, let alone human life. A few birds only."

Doc sat in his chair by the hearth, knitting, but he'd stopped. His head tilted up; his glasses flickered gold.

Snow watched as all the men paid close attention to each other, and every detail Hap gave them.

They were worried. Snow wasn't the only one. But they'd also found nothing.

Snow thought again that he could have seen an afterimage from his momentary sun blindness. He wanted to believe that. That he'd seen only a shape that his mind interpreted as human. But he couldn't. He still saw that perfect human shape imprinted into his thoughts, dark and slim, head up and forward. Cloaked. Staring at him. He saw two arms poking out of the cloak. The cloak had been thigh-length, which gave Snow the view of two legs silhouetted perfectly against the white backdrop of frost and drifts.

"I could have imagined it," Snow said, trying to appease the situation. And to comfort Sleepy, who remained tense at his side.

Doc's blond eyebrows scrunched together. "Maybe," he said.

"I don't want you all worrying about me. I'm safe here. You said it yourselves, no one knows I'm here."

"At any rate," Doc said, "you aren't to go outside without one of us with you at all times."

"That's fine. I'm liable to get lost anyway," Snow said, smiling to ease the tension.

Sneezy dropped himself into a chair and rocked back, tea cup to his lips.

Hap sauntered to the back room, taking off his cloak in a swirl as he went. He made extreme, exuberant gestures all the time, his energy always high, and Snow could not help but love him for it.

All these men surrounded Snow with love. And had vowed to keep him safe.

How did he deserve it?

"I want to help around here," Snow finally said. "Do something, anything to repay you all."

"You're still healing," Doc replied, taking up his knitting again.

"I'm getting better fast. I promise I'll help. Do anything. I can clean. I can do laundry while you're all at the quarry. I'll work. I'll cook. If Dope and Bash and Sneezy will teach me."

Sleepy turned to face Snow. "Hey, I can cook, too. I'll teach you."

Cheeks heating, Snow said, "All right. You can teach me, then."

"You burn the bread," Dope complained.

"I do not!"

"And the stew," Bash contributed.

"No, it was just that one time. It stuck to the bottom of the pot," Sleepy protested.

"More than one time," Sneezy said. He smiled innocently.

"Don't listen to them," Sleepy said to Snow. "I make a great rabbit stew."

"I believe you," Snow said, patting his arm.

Snow grinned. He loved them all. He wished he knew more about them, but didn't dare pry. And his own truth? For now, it needed to stay a secret.

The winter apple pies, made from Calville apples Hans the farmer had dried and stored, sat before them on the table tempting them with a fine dessert. But they would wait until after their supper.

These men had rules. And one was to keep an order to things or they'd all be living, as Dope had muttered more than once, like pigs.

Dope had chopped up some potatoes fine as he could and was frying potato cakes over the fire in a long-handled pan filled with lard. They sizzled.

The bread was sliced and warming, wrapped in oilcloth and buried in the ashes. They would also have boiled, fresh farm eggs. And there was vegetable soup. And slices of sharp cheese.

There were two pots, one for coffee, one for tea, both filled.

Snow warmed his hands on his own cup of coffee sweetened with pinches of sugar and a dollop of milk.

The men talked and the cooks shared the chores. Sneezy played a game of solitaire on the dining table. Doc continued to knit. Bash sat against Doc's knees reading a book by the firelight, checking on the soup every now and again.

Snow sat mesmerized by it all, Sleepy beside him trimming candle-ends with a pocketknife.

After a while, Snow got up.

Sleepy jumped to his side, his chair almost falling backward.

"I don't need your help. I can walk."

Sleepy sat back down, making a wry face with his lips pursed.

For the first time since he'd arrived, Snow limped by himself to the back of the cave to the water closet.

He passed the large, back room slowly, taking in all the details of it, now that he wasn't being carried. Or crawling along the floor petrified with fear.

Six beds, nice-sized, lined up close together in threes. Each had a simple headboard made of wood, and all the beds had ample furs and blankets and pillows for warmth. Four of the six beds were neatly made. Two remained rumpled.

Snow thought he could easily take care of that problem by helping to keep house while the men worked on the weekdays.

He peered at the chests at the foot of each bed. One was open and he saw inside folded clothing, scarves, and a leather belt. Beside each chest stood extra pairs of boots for each man. Pegs on the hearthside rock wall held cloaks and hats and what looked like a dressing gown or two.

Between each bed was a nightstand. One was stacked with books. Another held candle-ends. Yet another showed off several carved wooden toys: a deer, a wolf, a squirrel.

On a rack between two beds, clothing draped: shirts, trousers, under shorts all drying from a hasty morning launder.

The air smelled of lye tempered with lemon.

For a dank cave, it was quite cozy. Each man had a warm place to sleep, to live, to be. And they had each other.

Hand-woven rugs lay scattered about the floor. They would cushion bare feet in winter from the cold, hard ground.

Beyond the room, toward the slope-ceilinged back, water continued to drip into pots from above, a quiet slosh of liquid like a gentle rain.

Beyond that, in the darkness, the water closet stood. There was almost no light to see by, and Snow should have thought to bring a candle, but he could make out the wooden structure for privacy, and the dried hanging flowers and herbs. And he could see within the structure all he needed to accomplish his task.

Once done, he congratulated himself. Silly, perhaps, but it was the first time he'd peed without having to be carried or catered to with a chamber pot. It was a huge leap from how he'd been last weekend.

Back in the bedroom, his thoughts about who these men were and how they lived deepened. Snow thought of them as intrinsic to earth—earth-spirits—to life itself spilling outward despite cold and eternal winters and winds that swept the mountains without heart. They were like dream-souls come to life right out of his deepest wishes. And here he was with them, though odd-man out, but taken in, cared for, accepted.

His view from his tower prison had not encompassed them. He'd dreamed of rescue, but had forgotten men like this could exist. For Snow, they were only a dream. He had only occasional sparrows and a square of sky to be seen through the thick walls where the bars were deeply inlaid. And if he'd tilted his head just right, his view included valley ridges and tree-lines, a distant sparkle of a river, and squares of endless fields which bore crops only during the summer months.

He had not been able to see any villages or towns. They were to the east and west.

And where these men lived, north of the White Hills and further up toward the silvery mountains, he'd been blind.

On his way back to the front room, Snow stopped in the bedroom, turning around, breathing it all in. The six lovely beds. Why was the one in the front room set apart? Had they moved it just for him, or did Sleepy prefer to be aloof?

It did not seem that Sleepy was shy or unfamiliar with the men. But it was one more mystery for Snow to ponder.

The divider that Doc had used to give Snow privacy by the side of his bed was set up between the back bedroom and the front side area where Sleepy's bed was. Another divider closed the back room off from the front. Perhaps the first divider wasn't always there, and Sleepy's bed was pushed back to be more in line with the others.

Snow turned and could see the hearth from where he stood at the edge of the divider. He could see the chairs and the men. As he watched them unseen, Sleepy lifted his head from his candle wax carving and turned to look at him. Their eyes met and Sleepy smiled.

Snow smiled in return and moved back into the light and warmth and activity.

"Dinner's ready," called Dope.

Bash put his book aside. Doc set his yarn into his basket.

Even Sil the cat came at the call.

Sneezy tilted his chair forward and poured himself more tea.

Sleepy brushed the wax shavings from his spot and stored the candle-ends in a box at his feet.

Everything was hot and fresh. The flavors popped. Hot soup. Fresh bread. Boiled eggs with salt and pepper. But the best thing was the potato cakes. Snow ate four but it was all right. Dope had made stacks of them.

Snow felt almost too stuffed for pie.

Hap said, "There are eight of us. We can cut the first pie into eighths and each have a piece. Then save the other pies for dinner later."

"Good idea," said Doc.

They were all so full from the meal that there was no dissention.

The first taste of sweet apple within golden crust was like a miracle to Snow's taste buds. A bit of sugar, a bit of spice, it tasted of summer night, autumn wind.

"Hans sure knows how to bake," Hap said, rubbing his flat stomach.

Bash nodded. "So good."

The others grunted, still chewing. Metal spoons scraped against wooden plates.

When they finished, the plates and utensils were all stacked for cleaning. Dope did the washing up as well, using a pot of water and a wet rag to clean the dishes, then stacking them on a smaller table in a wooden rack.

Everyone sat around the table content, full, sipping coffee or tea.

Then Doc got out the rum.

Lots of grins spread across eager faces.

They did not pour the rum into mugs. Instead, they all shared the bottle, passing it around the table.

Snow took a hefty sip and felt the liquid spread fire through his stomach and limbs. It soothed as it went, chasing every fear and tense thought into oblivion.

The bottle was passed around several times and the room began to fill with energetic, happy chatter. Eyes glistened. Cheeks turned red.

Snow laughed at the men's silly tales and anecdotes. Of the quarry. Of the woods. Of the village where they shopped for goods, and of the people they met within. They spoke also of the farm that Hans ran.

After a while, Snow's eyelids drooped.

Sleepy suggested a nap.

Snow felt like a child. But then the rest of the men thought it a great idea as well. And several of them shuffled off to snatch an hour's sleep before more chores and the preparation of dinner.

Snow carefully set his borrowed boots by the side of the bed, and folded his pretty red cloak and placed it and his new knit cap at the foot of the mattress.

He kept on his woolen socks, no doubt knitted by Doc himself. Then he curled up under the furs.

Distantly, he felt Sleepy climb in beside him at his back. Moments later, Snow fell asleep.

Chapter Twelve

Snow woke in the night, dreaming of that wonderful apple pie he'd had at both dinner and supper.

Under the furs with Sleepy, he was toasty warm.

The hearth burned golden and low. The soft weight of Sil sleeping pressed between his and Sleepy's feet.

A whisper came by Snow's ear.

"Are you awake?"

"Yes." Snow's whisper came out faint.

"I just want you to know I believe in you."

Snow smiled. He felt real to himself, but maybe not to Sleepy? "What do you mean?"

"That you saw someone in the wood."

"Oh."

"On my honor, I promise to be more vigilant. To protect you with my life," said Sleepy.

"You already are. You see to my every need. Sleepy, you are my knight. You know that, right?"

Sleepy let out a fast breath, like a short laugh. "I like when you say that. But you give me too much credit. I've done nothing more than help a man in need."

"Which is saying a lot. It's everything. Some people are not good like that, like you all are. Some people do not seem to understand or even know the right way to live. Some people are just not good." Snow let his whisper fade away.

"What happened to you, Snow?"

Snow pressed his lips tightly together, not answering.

Finally, he whispered, "How did you come to be here, Sleepy?"

"These are very personal questions. I know." Sleepy tucked himself tighter against Snow's back.

"Yes." Snow sighed.

"I'll tell you if you tell me. A trade."

Snow said, "I'm not sure."

"You're not ready."

"No. I'm not ready for a lot of things. But I need to be. I need to grow up. Fast. Or I will never find my way in the world. Ever."

"You are finding your way. You're here, right? Not imprisoned anymore."

"But I would be dead if not for you all."

Sleepy shifted, slipping his arm under Snow's shoulders. "I would be, too, if not for Doc and Hap and Bash, who saved me from dying of cold. I was homeless."

"Yes, you told me that. You were fighting for your life like me?" Snow asked.

Sleepy nodded against Snow's shoulder. They were skin to skin. A slow burn began deep in Snow's belly. Sleepy's thighs rested against the backs of his own. At the small of his back, Snow felt such heat. He often thought he felt the press of Sleepy's erection when they woke like this each morning, but couldn't be sure. Sleepy kept himself in check, always non-forceful and gentlemanly. Right now he felt the heat, but nothing more.

Did Sleepy want him as much as Snow wanted Sleepy? He thought yes, of course, but Snow still felt guilty for thinking such things. He couldn't help it. The world was a crazy place and he did not see how he could stay here with these men indefinitely. But the more he fell for Sleepy, the more he could not imagine ever being without him.

Snow took a deep breath, then leaned back into Sleepy, the skin of his shoulder blades brushing Sleepy's chest, his elbow knocking lightly into ribs. Sleepy's chin moved over Snow's head. His hand came up and he touched Snow's hair just above the temple.

"What?" Sleepy whispered.

"I want to tell you. I do. But I don't want my story to put any of you in more danger because of me."

"All right."

"I was imprisoned by the queen."

"At the Palace of the White Hills?"

"Yes."

"For how long?"

"Two years."

"Oh, sweetheart…"

The words soared through Snow's chest and into his mind in swirling affection. Arms tightened about him. Snow felt his eyes begin to sting.

Sleepy cared. He cared so much. And he didn't truly know who Snow was.

"Grump was in the dungeons there for a while. Sneezy, too. It's where they met."

"Really?"

"It's their story to tell. But yes."

"I didn't do anything bad. I'm not a bad person," Snow said.

"You couldn't possibly be a bad person. I could never think it. A lot of men are unfairly imprisoned, especially in the past ten years."

"The old lady—I mean the queen is cruel."

Sleepy nodded against Snow's head. "Her guard is made up of the most vicious men. They have taken babies from their mother's arms on the queen's command."

"She wants all power and no dissent whatsoever," Snow said. "Not even a word against her. I think she's quite mad."

"Yes, her methods do cause quite a bit of harm. It does make for quite a gloomy realm which is why men like us live more in the wild."

"But you have had your run-ins with the queen's guard," Snow said. "You said that was why you were out in the night when you all found me."

"Yes, we have. But we steer clear and try to keep things peaceful. They wanted money that night, and we gave it."

"I'm sorry."

"It happens. Some people can't fight back, or have no money. Their fate is determined on a whim by those warriors. It's a sad kingdom to live in at the moment."

"I was kept away from the world. I didn't know how bad things were." Snow could not have done anything about it, but he had had no clue the old lady was as decadent and cruel beyond the palace walls as well. He had thought perhaps she only hated him because he was the rightful heir, and for no other reason. The only thing she had ever seemed to want from him was an heir of her own with royal blood, but for reasons he did not know, that had never happened. Maybe she was barren. Maybe he was. But he was grateful there was no child who had to endure her abuse.

84

Snow's body tightened at the memory.

Sleepy said, "The bad is difficult to put out of the mind. It takes over, creates sickness. The worst thing for it is to be alone. Which is why we have each other. Doc has made sure we stick together. All of us."

Snow realized he'd probably said too much. There was no going back on it, though. He had said he was imprisoned by the queen. They all knew his name was Snow. If Sleepy didn't now guess he was the dead boy-prince, only not really dead, Snow had seriously misjudged his intelligence.

"I—I—had it pretty hard. But I think I've said too much. By now you must know." He shut his eyes against a beginning burn.

"Know what?" Sleepy asked.

"Who I am. I mean, because of my name. And what I've said." He whispered the words so softly he thought Sleepy had not heard him. He swallowed hard, throat starting to ache with emotion. Fear. Shame. Worry about endangering his new friends.

After a long pause, Sleepy put his arm over Snow's naked waist, just grazing, barely touching. "You are a winter flower who has finally found a little bit of sun so it can finally bloom. That's what you are."

At the words, Snow burst into tears, suddenly gasping. The hot liquid flamed over the bridge of his nose and along one temple. His lashes grew thick and sticky as he tried to blink away the storm.

"Now, you see?" Sleepy's breath and voice went directly into Snow's ear. "You are not alone anymore. Bad is out there, yes, but it can't get into your heart as long as you have people who love you. As long as you allow yourself to love. Doc taught me that, a lesson I sorely needed."

Snow pressed the side of his face hard into the pillow. Sleepy raised his arm from Snow's waist and pressed his palm into Snow's hair. His cheek pressed there, too, and he held him like that until Snow's breathing calmed.

"How long have you known about me?" Snow's whisper came out harsh with residual tears.

"Since the night we saved your life, my lord."

My lord.

Snow's skin heated, then chilled. All this time! And they had already known.

"Why—why didn't you say anything?"

"Trust runs both ways," Sleepy said. "We weren't sure how you would react if you thought we knew you were someone other than a mere stranger along the way. And we couldn't know if you were a victim or player in the queen's evil tricks."

"But how did you know? I thought the realm believed me dead?"

"Rumors abound. We had always believed you might be alive. Guards get drunk in pubs. They talk. The underground believed you could be held apart and isolated in the tower, but it was gossip, rumor."

"But people suspected?"

"And some are even ready to rally for you upon confirmation of your survival. You did not realized, did you, Prince Snow, that you have never really been alone in all these years?"

More silent tears pressed from behind Snow's eyelids. *All these years.*

Since his father remarried, the king had continued on in the palace with his usual routine of education and attending royal functions. He was not a threat to the old lady as long as he held no power. But she kept him indoors, alone. Apart from any who might be loyal to him. She ordered him about. But even then, Sleepy was saying, Snow had not been alone.

The queen garnered all the attention. He didn't know people actually *wanted* him as their next king, only that he was the heir by blood whether they supported him or not.

The old lady put lies into his head, telling him he wasn't wanted or liked, that people didn't care about him, and they'd need a stronger, better ruler than a little boy figurehead waiting to turn eighteen. Snow's father was absent from these meetings, and when he did see his son, passive. As if he had gone daft in the head.

Snow had believed her cruel words. She'd cut off his ability to mingle with the public, disallowed him any travel outside the palace.

Unofficially, he'd been her prisoner for far more than two years. Her mental cruelty to him had been just as bad as the physical.

If not for his rescuers, he would have been dead, and no one the wiser.

Sleepy kept petting him until he calmed.

"You've been hurt badly, but I hope not irreparably," Sleepy told him.

Snow lifted his chin. He chastised himself. He had no right to be crying so pitifully in Sleepy's arms. Each one of these men had suffered as well. He did not know their stories yet, but he vowed he would. They had been hurt and Doc had eventually brought them all together. If they could heal, so could he.

Snow turned onto his back and in the dim hearth-light saw Sleepy looking down at him, his hair hanging forward around his beautiful face, the whites of his eyes catching the light. The rest of him was in shadow, but Snow could smell him, pine and autumn, sweet and alluring.

Snow lifted his arm and touched Sleepy's bare shoulder. "You've been hurt, too. All of you have suffered. I am selfish to believe I'm the only victim of the old—of Serena."

"You are not selfish. You have only just entered this world and you are learning. Quickly learning."

Snow sniffed once. He bit hard at his lower lip and said, "What if I told you I love it here. And I never want to leave."

Sleepy laughed under his breath. "I love it, too. We've made this a home."

"Comfortable, peaceful, safe."

"Yes. It is. But we all have learned from Doc the right way to live, and if a bigger deed calls any of us away, we would have to follow that call."

"But how if you don't have the means?"

"We have some means. There are others like us. We are secret and not just a few. And we are lucky that you came along when you did and we could help you. Lucky as can be."

Snow had never felt lucky. Privileged, yes. At least when he was young. But he'd known nothing else. When he became aware of the old lady's mean-streak, though, he'd counted himself less than charmed and explicitly not favored.

Sleepy's words settled into him. Slowly, he realized what Sleepy was saying. *We are secret and not just a few.* There were people on Snow's side, then. An underground. A resistance? And why not? Serena had clearly tortured the land and its people. That behavior created the very resistance she feared.

Snow decided maybe he was lucky after all. He was still among the living. There was that. And there were people who actually thought about him, wanted him to be alive so they had a prince they could back. Maybe he'd still be only a figurehead, but anything had to be better than the current ruling queen.

Sleepy's thigh was tight and hot against his, his arm over Snow's chest, fingers splayed along the side of his head. That, even more than the information he'd just been given, spun his head. His body became tight with need. Want. Desire.

Sleepy, his own fantasy prince come to save him, now in the flesh.

In a soft whisper, Snow said, "I want to know you. All of you. Your whole story."

Sleepy's grin flashed in the dimness. "Got time to be bored?"

"No. I'll be fascinated, no matter what you tell me."

Sleepy laughed. A soft whisper of amusement. They had been hushed and sober and teary and chuckling this whole time in their cocoon of furs. From his shoulders to his now only slightly aching feet, a sudden warmth melted through Snow, igniting his veins.

Everything about this man made him want to be closer to him. Physically and emotionally. But would Sleepy want him in return now that he was sure who Snow really was?

"Sleepy?" Snow pushed his palm across the man's shoulder and up the side of his neck. "Will you kiss me?"

Sleepy's fingers slid up through Snow's hair and the low light in the hearth trembled. Snow's eyes were wide open as he saw Sleepy's shadowy head lower to him, and he felt the man's body adjust to the gesture, a trembling weight against his thigh, hip, ribs and chest.

"I thought you'd never ask."

Snow lay very still, his lips parting slightly.

Soft lips brushed his, the brief, teasing touch sending canes of coppery light through Snow's peripheral vision. The tease left him wanting, a space of air between their mouths, then Sleepy's lips brushed over him again and pressed down and this time they did not leave and Snow's entire being brimmed with elation. He could not suppress a small groan muffled by Sleepy's perfect kiss.

Snow had only had forced sex, his single experience with such things in his life, but never ever had he been kissed. For that matter, it crossed his mind that the old lady's antics did not even count as sex. They were something else entirely.

Therefore, he'd never experienced willing sex, or making love, or anything like that before.

Sleepy's mouth was soft against his own. His hand caressed Snow's head. His chest pressed against Snow's. Hearts hammered. Snow loved the feel of him, and stretched his body, lifting up to press himself into Sleepy.

He grew aroused quickly, body straining to love, join, *be* with this man.

Sleepy's mouth opened. The kiss deepened. Snow caught quick breaths through his nose, pulled back once, gasping, then re-initiated the kiss, delving shyly with his tongue.

Sleepy met his tongue with his own and an ecstatic dance began.

After a minute, Sleepy dragged his mouth to Snow's cheek, jaw, chin. Kissing him all over his face.

"You're so beautiful," Sleepy kept whispering between kisses.

Snow thought: *I am yours. I am yours.*

He would do anything for Sleepy. Give him the world if he could.

He turned so his body matched Sleepy's better and felt Sleepy's erection slide across his hip, strong and hard.

The beauty of Sleepy was hard to forget. Snow had an image of him etched into his mind, bathing in the mornings surrounded by the warmth of the hearth, the tall strength, broad shoulders, flex of muscle in his back and flanks and buttocks. And that proud cock, always half hard and bobbing as he washed, the tip pink slightly protruding from his golden foreskin. The balls were tight and dark and firm, pressing against the base of the jutting cock. So pretty.

Now Snow could feel that cock, how firm it was against his own skin, how manly, and he wanted more.

He trembled with need, and Sleepy's body answered. Before Snow could plan what he wanted next, they were moving together, sliding together in a graceful undulation and Snow's cock bobbed up and then was trapped between them.

The friction against his erection came from Sleepy's hip and abdomen until they moved together and their cocks met in pure euphoria.

Snow had only asked for a kiss, but he wanted it all. He didn't stop himself. He couldn't.

"Sleepy," he whispered, and the lips, which had delved just below his jaw, came back to his mouth and pressed down until Snow opened again and their tongues dueled.

It was like so many things his mind could not contain. Like becoming fire. Like melting into the skin and bone and spirit of another being until there was no separation, one from the other. Like creating through song or painting or poetry a new existence but with their bodies.

In this time, nothing else seemed real but touch and pleasure and love. Two men moving in the deep of a chilly May night under the furs. Two spirits connecting.

They slipped and slid together, mouths locked, until Sleepy lifted himself a bit and stole his hand between them. With a smooth sureness, he grasped their cocks together and milked them.

Snow was already on the verge of coming, a bright climb to heights of dizzying pleasure like he'd never known. The extra pressure finished him, and he gasped, holding back his cries so as not to wake the other men. Over and over his breath caught and expelled as his cock throbbed with his release.

As he became aware again, he felt Sleepy stiffen over him, let out a long breath, and more wetness spread between them.

Sleepy rubbed it all over their bellies until it no longer felt wet, just a little sticky, and then reached to grasp Snow to him with both arms, pulling him to his side until they were face to face.

Snow's arms came around Sleepy's firm waist.

They kissed some more for a long time. Snow became lethargic with pleasure, eyes closed, mind spinning.

Sleepy pulled him to his chest and kissed his forehead. "Sleep now," he said.

"Don't let go," Snow murmured.

"Never." He ran a hand up and down Snow's back. "We'll talk more in the morning. For now, rest without a worry."

Snow drifted off, safe in the dauntless arms of love.

Chapter Thirteen

Sunday morning was for sleeping in again.

Snow grasped Sleepy hard, as they repeated their middle of the night lovemaking session, rubbing, kissing, groaning to the sounds of some of the other men making love in the big bedroom.

He could not get enough of Sleepy. He wrapped his legs around him, pulling him closer, weaving his fingers into his wavy, silken hair. He touched his palms to Sleepy's cheeks and jaw with unshaven morning beard, traced his lips, then kissed them.

Sleepy grew bold and sucked one of Snow's fingers into his mouth. When he did that, Snow came with a gasp over his stomach, and Sleepy drew him in for a kiss, saying, "Beautiful, so beautiful," into his open mouth.

Snow reached between them and grasped Sleepy's big, throbbing cock in his hand, not surprised by the weight of it, but loving how it felt. He gently milked it until Sleepy spurted with a soft groan onto his fingers and against their bodies.

Was Sleepy being quiet for Snow's sake? They weren't sneaking around. The others knew they slept together every night, and they wore no sleep garments, and this morning they had to have heard them.

But Sleepy was a gentleman through and through and he kept himself quiet, their love private for now, theirs to share alone, the two of them as one.

They rested together, faces close, lips nearly touching so that they breathed each other's air.

Snow dozed while little surges of ecstasy continued to ignite him. He could envision himself wanting Sleepy again and again. All the time. He would not be able to do anything without the thought of him.

When Sleepy finally rose, this time Snow rose with him.

Naked, Sleepy approached the hearth and built it up, bending and flexing his bronze body. Snow could not take his eyes off him. Sleepy put a pot of water on the hook to heat.

He turned.

Snow had grabbed the red cloak about his shoulders but had not fastened it in front.

Sleepy stared at him, smiling. "Let me bathe you," he said.

Snow came forward to stand by the hearth. His bound feet ached less today, and his balance was good. It was wonderful to be able to walk again, to be able to go about the house without being carried. Though he'd loved it when Sleepy carried him.

The water heated quickly, warm for washing, and Sleepy used a thick, quilted glove to grab the water pot and set it on the bricks before the hearth. He took a cloth and soaked it in the warm water, then brought it to Snow's body.

Snow pushed the cloak back until the red wool fell behind him, exposing his body to Sleepy.

Sleepy washed him all over, gentle and loving. The water left his skin sweetly chilled, but the hearth was warm, and Snow didn't shiver. He grew hot and hotter.

Snow burned for him to do this, bathe him with the soft, warm cloth, and his cock filled again.

Sleepy stood to wash Snow's chest and neck. He fastened the cloak at the neck, then pushed it back further, exposing Snow's shoulders, and washed him there and up his neck, behind his ears, and over his cheeks. There might have been dried tears there, and there certainly was dried semen on his belly, all gone now.

Sleepy knelt again and the last thing he did was wash Snow's cock, which was hard again and waving.

Snow could not contain himself. He started to back away, but Sleepy gripped his hips and leaned in, taking Snow's cock all the way into his mouth.

Snow gasped, whispering, "Not in front of everyone. They'll see!"

"Hmm." Sleepy's hum was low, soft, and to solve the problem he brought the edges of the cloak around Snow's hips and hid his head and Snow's lower body in the folds of it.

The mouth on Snow's cock moved up and down, milking with firm lips, sucking, licking, taking the tip firmly in a deep kiss and licking the head back and forth, up and down. Sleepy moved down again, sucking hard, the velvet of his mouth encasing his head and the shaft.

Nervous, Snow looked about but no one had gotten up yet.

He shut his eyes and let himself be taken over again by pleasure. By Sleepy's infectious love.

He was young. And Sleepy was very good at this sort of act. In no time, Snow felt himself soar up until he could soar no more, and his cock exploded, pulsing into Sleepy's mouth.

Sleepy sucked him, swallowing and swallowing, making Snow so lust-crazy that his cock continued to throb.

When Sleepy let him go, Snow was clean. Not a drop was spilled. Sleepy rubbed his cheek against the now softening penis, kissing the tip twice, then reached for the wet cloth and pail. As if nothing had happened, not the most sacred, phenomenal thing in the world, Sleepy cleaned Snow's cock and balls, washed his thighs again, then stood and took the cloth to wash himself.

Still trying to catch his breath, Snow grasped the cloth. "Let me."

A perfect body stood before Snow. Naked and unabashed.

Snow walked around him, the cloak catching on his forearms, and stopped at Sleepy's back. Muscular and magnificent, it seemed a good place to start.

He washed Sleepy all over, reveling in the firm curves and planes of the man, enjoying the opportunity to explore him everywhere. He loved touching the rounded buttocks and the divots at their sides where leg met hip, the strong thighs, the flat stomach and the broad chest. Sleepy smelled like spring, all damp and warm in the flickering firelight.

When Snow came to the lovely cock and balls, he gently washed the springy flesh, watching it rise, and was himself stirred by the pink head peaking at him from the tip.

Snow looked up. "I want to make you come again."

Sleepy put a hand on his shoulder. "Tonight we will. For now, everything is as it should be. And the others are starting to rise."

They'd heard the sounds of sighing, gasping, and whispered begging. The others had participated in their own pleasures, even if subdued for the sake of their guest.

And then Snow had a lovely thought of what might have gone on here before he arrived, if they all shared in mutual bathing and pleasure before the fire, seven naked men, seven hard cocks all waiting their turn for whoever wanted to give pleasure, and whoever wanted to receive.

Could it have been like that? Had his presence interfered with their privacy, their mysterious relationships with each other?

Snow reached up and put his hands on Sleepy's wide shoulders. He tugged him down for a kiss before the fire, soft and slow.

When he pulled back, he said not another word. He went back to their bed, gathered his clothes, and began to dress with the cloak still on, hiding his body.

He heard footsteps, murmurs. The other men were dressing, or coming out to the hearth to bathe.

Snow turned, wearing his trousers and shirt, just as pans began to clatter, cups to clink. He saw Doc fully dressed, bending to feed Sil. He saw Bash put a pot over the fire to heat. And Dope, though shirtless, had started to get out the makings for his porridge.

Snow wanted to help but couldn't think what to do. So he stood and watched the beauty of the men in motion, looking at the life they'd made, envying their ease.

Sleepy had put on trousers and held his shirt across his forearm. He looked up at Snow and smiled, eyebrows raised.

Snow came toward him into the light.

*

Snow licked the last of the meal from his spoon and set it on the table beside his bowl. His borrowed bowl. For nothing here was his, yet everything had been generously given to him as if he were a brother. As if he deserved it. Clothing, medical aid, food, a bed to sleep in, and a generous and protective lover.

He looked around the table at these men, these few supporters left over from when the king, Snow's father, had ruled. These secret rebels, anti-queen advocates, hidden supporters for the true heir to the throne itself, Prince Snow of the White Hills.

Snow drew a breath. His heart thumped against the walls of his chest.

"I—I have something to say to you all."

The men looked up. Some had finished eating and were politely waiting for everyone to finish before they got up to start their day, do the chores, or spend leisure time relaxing, reading, playing cards. Or knitting.

Snow was awkward to have all their attention him, but he pushed through his fears and spoke. He was, after all, a prince.

"I first want to thank you all for everything you have done for me. I can never repay you."

The men made various dissenting sounds and gestures.

Snow continued. "I was pretty sick, not thinking clearly, and my life up to now has been restricted. I was rarely allowed out of my prison cell, and only then to—" He faltered.

"Queen Serena imprisoned me. I am not dead as rumors would have the realm believe. Of course, I realized you all had figured it out. My name, Snow, is uncommon even around these White Hills. And my age, my hair, well, you all know my identity. I thought hiding it from you might protect you, and when I was well I would go away and you would not have to know, not have my problems becomes yours, and if ever questioned by the queen's guard, you could honestly say that you had no idea you helped her stepson, Prince Snow, escape the huntsman she had ordered to assassinate him."

Snow glanced at Sleepy and continued.

"But now I am informed you already knew. That you suspected I was alive, and that you are part of a faction who supports me. I'm so very very grateful. I would never have guessed in a thousand years that others gave any thought to me, that's how locked away from the real world I was."

As Snow looked about, he saw the men had no reactions of surprise at his words. Only concern and sympathy, and glints of held back outrage in their eyes.

Doc leaned forward, elbows on the table. "We are all fortunate that you have survived such harsh conditions. For you are our true prince who should be king."

Snow glanced again at each of their faces, including Sleepy, who watched him with a sad smile.

To hear Doc say the words nearly overwhelmed Snow. For Doc was Doc. Snow saw him as the leader. The one who kept these men together. The glue. To Snow, Doc was everything, the center of this world. Snow was nothing.

But the words rang through the room. *Our true prince who should be king.*

Snow bowed his head. He might have been neglected, but he'd still been raised and taught as prince. Snow's father had been a good man before the old lady came and caused him to be passive around her. Those early parental influences, when the realm enjoyed better days, remained. "A true king is a servant to his people, to their needs, making for them the best life he can. No matter what happens, you seven—I shall always be the one to bow before you."

Dope laughed. "I never had a king bow to me before."

Grump said, but with a half-smile, "Ah, you say such idealistic platitudes because you are young. But no matter, I still support you."

Bash said, "I think he means it. He's speaking true to his heart, you daft idiots."

"Enough," Sleepy said, coming like a snake striking out of his placid silence. "He's not the king yet. And we don't have a firm plan. So we continue to protect him."

"Bide our time?" asked Sneezy.

"Yes." Sleepy crossed his arms over his chest.

"I don't know how I can ever beat the queen," Snow said. "But I thank you all for trying and for your support. Whatever happens, you are my true brothers. Always."

Doc pushed his specs higher up his nose. "We do need time, that is not in question. But not to raise an army."

"We have warriors," Hap said. "But no organization."

"We have the truth. We need to get the truth out," Doc said. "That will help speed things along."

"But if the truth gets out," Sleepy argued, "someone will find Snow. They'll hunt him even more intensely, high and low. We may live in the hills, but our existence is no secret. We work at the quarry. We trade with Hans. We go into the village at least once week. Everyone will be interrogated. Every home searched. Even ours."

Doc looked very patient, the fire reflecting scarlet in his blond hair. "Snow can be disguised. Snow can become one of us. It's not far-fetched. Who would know him on sight these days? If we hide his hair—"

"Only the queen and her most trusted guards who kept me locked in the tower would recognize me," Snow agreed.

"And the huntsman," Sleepy added. "If he is alive."

"Yes. He would know me, too."

"Still," Doc said. "I think we need to let the factions know the prince is alive and well. There must be truth to aid an uprising. You would have all the people, then, to stand against the queen and her guard."

"All of them?" Snow asked.

"I have little doubt of it. Those who are afraid will at first band with the queen. But it's only fear that will make them side with those they see as a threat. If more and more people learn the truth, the queen's power will subside. She'll be seen as the mere figurehead she is with bullies to pillage her lands for her gain."

"But those bullies have numbers and weapons and power," Grump said. "There is no way to fight them and win without our own army. We have factions, but not enough numbers."

"We can if we can turn some of those bullies, even if only a few."

"And how do you propose we do that?" Hap asked.

"The queen's guard is not without its unhappy complainers among the ranks." Low and quiet, Doc's voice always calmed whoever he was around. Along with healing, keeping the peace among men who might otherwise have digressed into scarred and angry souls was Doc's gift. Snow noted this with much admiration. For Doc had literally saved him with his physician skills.

"For now," Doc continued, "we need to hide and protect Prince Snow."

"Please, just call me Snow." Snow was awkward with the title. With his secret revealed.

"Yes. It's best. We must be in the habit of never referring to him as the prince for anyone who might overhear while we are away from home."

The others all nodded their agreement.

"And—and you must treat me normal," Snow said. "I want to contribute. I will learn to cook, clean, do whatever you need. I want to learn."

Bash said, "But a prince should not do these things!"

"He should have fine things," Dope agreed. "And servants."

"He's one of us," Doc said. "A human being. What's in your head are roles played at levels that have nothing to do with reality as we are living it right now."

Snow smiled. "I wish to be one of you. More than anything. Please, I don't want you to think of me as a prince. I'll clean the hearth. I'll wipe the tables and wash the linens. And I'll do it with my heart full because without all of you, I wouldn't be here. I wouldn't have found this beautiful, safe place. For me, this home you have created is more utopian than any castle or riches."

They had talked about this before, but so far no one had begun to teach Snow anything.

Bash said, "Oh, all right. I'll teach you how to make miner's stew."

Dope pushed back his coppery bangs. "And porridge."

Hap laughed. "My bed linens do need a good washing."

Sneezy wiped his sleeve across his nose. "I'll show you how all the dishware is stored."

Grump's brows narrowed to a single line. "What about cleaning the latrine?"

"I'll do that, too," Snow said quickly, unfazed.

"I'll do that," Dope said.

Snow turned to look at him. "It's not beneath me to clean what I use."

Sleepy looked down, then up. "You shouldn't—" he started to say.

Avoiding Snow's gaze, he looked at all the others. "He's still our guest. Either I or Dope will clean the water closet. No arguments."

Snow smiled softly. His cheeks heated because Sleepy was so protective, so good. He wanted to spoil Snow, and his love glowed like a bright light all around him. The cave walls glimmered.

There was more talk, lighter, easy as the subject changed to the day's routine.

Doc's brown eyes met Snow's as chatter filled the air. Gently, he nodded. Snow nodded back, his body feeling full and content, well-loved.

How he wished he could make this time last forever.

Chapter Fourteen

The cupboards were full of newly cleaned dishes. Embers and ash had been swept from the bricks by the hearth. The long wood table glistened from a fresh wipe-down.

The fire chattered merrily to itself. Night had fallen. The last of the apple pie, crumbs and all, had been eaten.

Seven men and one prince sat in a semi-circle by the fire, per Doc's request.

Snow settled next to Sleepy, their thighs touching.

"It's time to tell our stories, share our pasts with Snow, who may share his own as well." Doc said. "Snow? Would you like to start?"

But Snow shook his head, a sudden panic overtaking him. His skin flushed. His eyes teared up.

"I'll start," Sleepy said. Always protective. Like a true king's guard.

Snow turned to look at him, that dark gaze going somewhat distant, yet his features true and handsome. But something haunted him. Snow itched to take his hand but held himself very still instead.

Sleepy took a shallow breath, let it out, then another. He began, eyes on the center flames within the hearth, never looking at any of them, as if he were going into a place inside his mind of cold retreat, the only evidence of life remaining: his voice.

"I had a sister named Keri. I was not much younger than you are now. She was fourteen. I came to walk her home from the schoolhouse down the road from our farm, as we did every day when I was still school age and she was just a little girl. On our way down the road, I remember we found some wild lavender blooming under a tree. It was still cold. Snow in the hills. But these flowers were pushing their way to the sun, steadfast and beautiful after a long winter. She went to smell them, not to pick them. She wouldn't want to disturb their natural beauty, that's the kind of girl she was."

Sleepy took a deep breath, swallowing.

"We didn't see them at first. Coming up the road. I was distracted myself by a fox who stopped to gaze at me from deeper within the wood. He swished his red tail. Everything was so peaceful, and the sun was shining white and fierce. We were simply dawdling, enjoying a brief glance at spring peeking through winter's last days. Maybe if we'd seen them, we could have hidden. Like we had many times before. Not trusting. Always told by our parents to come straight home, quick as could be."

Sleepy blinked. Snow pushed his thigh tighter to him.

"The queen's guard came upon us fast, a mass of them, maybe two dozen on horseback. They drew up and demanded a tax for using the road. A road we'd always walked our whole lives. They insisted our parents must pay and followed us, forcing us ahead of them, to our farm. There, they took what they wanted. When my father offered food, while begging them to take nothing more since we had so little, they killed him and my mother without a thought. Right before our eyes. For trying to negotiate the tax, they said. The swords—" He stopped. Closed his eyes and continued. "The swords cut through them like a knife through butter. I froze, my back against the wall, Keri right beside me, her arms around my waist, hiding her face against my side as she silently wept. They ransacked the entire house, taking what they wanted, destroying what they left behind. Then they took my sister, grabbed her from my arms. Ignoring her screams, one guard tossed her over his shoulder and they took her away with them, laughing and making disrespectful remarks about her.

"I could do nothing. I had no weapons, no idea how to fight. And I was terrified.

"The farm was in ruins by the time they'd left. We had a cow, a pig and two horses. They took those for tax, as well. And the tools for planting. Everything. There must have been sixty men.

"After that, I had nothing.

"I made my way up into the hills, still terrified, planning to hide, or die. I actually did hope to die. I was in such grief I could not comprehend the world any longer.

"I made my way to the quarry. I wasn't really looking for work. I honestly didn't know where I was.

"Doc and Sneezy found me as they started home from their jobs. I was just off the path, lying in a drift. Waiting to freeze to death. I don't remember a lot of those first days. They brought me back here and Doc talked to me all night for many nights, putting my mind back together."

Sleepy opened his eyes. The fire flamed within the depths, which were dark as midnight now.

"To this day, I don't know if Keri is alive or dead. Surely they tortured her. Probably raped her. But did they kill her? I have no clue. I've been searching for her to this day with no leads and no results."

Snow was so shocked, he had no words. He realized his mouth was open, and he gazed at Sleepy as if seeing him for the first time.

"Thank you, Sleepy." Doc's soft voice broke the tension a bit. "I know that was hard. But we must share so Snow understands. We must make him understand."

Snow blinked back tears. He already understood. But before he could say anything, the next man began.

Bash bowed his head as he spoke, his dark hair hanging against his cheeks. "Doc found me, too."

He proceeded to tell a story much like Sleepy's, only his family had died of the red fever. They might have gotten help, but they couldn't afford medicine. Bash had caught the illness, too, but not as badly as the others. Still, in a stupor, he'd wandered off from the dead bodies of his parents, brothers and sisters until lost. The farm, a rich land that produced corn and alfalfa, considered abandoned, had been seized by royal command and now belonged to the ruling government, namely the queen.

More stories followed. Dope, an orphan from an early age, had been imprisoned in the queen's dungeons for two years for stealing a loaf of bread. A friendly guard let him go free after some time.

Dope found work at the quarry and Doc met him there, befriending the lonely boy who was just barely eighteen.

Hap also had a tragic past. For his lightheartedness, Snow never would have guessed he'd survived being bought as a child and made to work a brothel. He'd escaped eventually. He lived in the woods, camping, and also found work at the quarry where he, too, met Doc.

Sneezy and Grump had run with thieves in their early years, and had known each other since they were boys. They eventually bought and ran a farm. As lovers, they hid their relationship, but someone suspected anyway and they were turned in to the queen's guard and sentenced to death.

On the day they were both to be hanged, they were taken by two guards to an underground brothel to "have some fun with guys who like their holes buggered" before they were put to death.

Their luck was high that day as their guards drank themselves into stupors, leaving their bindings too loose, and Sneezy and Grump were able to escape.

The stories were dark, filled with murder, abuse, rape, kidnapping, prejudice.

Snow knew firsthand life could be ugly, but one after the other, the stories these men had survived drew terrible pictures of events that might have been avoided had the realm been run properly, with aid for poverty, sickness, and without the crimes committed by a royal guard out of control, taking anything they wanted from the land and its people.

When the stories ended, they had not yet heard from Doc. But all eyes turned to Snow.

Perhaps his tale was not as bad as theirs. He could not get such terrible images out of his mind. And he felt great guilt that as their prince he had been unable to do anything to protect them. If only he'd grown up a little faster, opened his eyes wider, and fought harder to learn of the outside world.

But buoyed by their camaraderie, and kind gazes, Snow finally found his words.

"My mother died when I was ten. Of course I loved her and missed her. But at least I still had food and clothes and schooling. Very soon, I had a step-mother who restricted my access to the outdoors, and only allowed me to attend official royal functions and otherwise ignored me, but I suffered nothing physically. I was only lonely. I did not know anything about the current realm. Until I turned eighteen."

His throat went drier and drier as he talked.

"I was given a purple cloak which had once been my father's. It was a birthday gift. I was to wear it at my coronation the following week. But that never happened. Only a day later, my father died. In the middle of one night, while I was sleeping, guards broke into my room and carried me up to the tower. There was one window with bars. And one thick door, always locked. I was left there for two years. I had no idea why, except that the old lady—I mean the queen was irrational in her whims, and wanted to retain her power."

Snow looked down at his hands which had scrunched together in his lap.

"She wanted a child. At sword point, she made me try to—" He coughed, then cleared his throat. "Made me try to get her pregnant. I don't know why she didn't use one of the guards, but it seemed important her child be of royal blood. I was all that was left."

Snow heard Sleepy take a few deep breaths as he continued with his story.

"She could never get with child, but she still tried. Once a month I was brought to her chamber. Once a month she was the only physical contact I had for two years."

"The queen raped you?" Grump asked.

"Shhh!" Doc held up his hand. "We are not to question. Only listen."

Snow could not look any of them in the eye. Softly, he said, "She is ill—or something. She kept saying to me, every time, 'Am I not the most beautiful person in all the land?' She had her chamber filled with mirrors. Something is very wrong with her, but I did not realize how far her madness extended into the land until now."

Snow lifted his head now that he was done. "Thank you for telling me all your stories. Now I know."

"Thank you for telling us yours."

"But Doc, you haven't told your own," Snow said hesitantly.

"You are quite right." His voice remained low and calm. "I grew up quite wealthy and privileged. I trained in the western lands at university to be a physician. I opened an office with great success. I married and we had a beautiful daughter. When she was three, she went missing. Everyone in town looked for her. Three weeks later, her badly tortured body was found by a riverbed."

Snow could not believe he was hearing yet another horrible story. But this was nothing to do with the queen, simply a dark misfortune to happen to the kindest of men.

"My wife could not handle the tragedy and its details. We grieved, but her grief consumed her and one day when I was away, she left the house. She went to the river when our daughter's body was found and tied rocks to her limbs, then jumped in and drowned herself.

"I finally heard that the two men who did this terrible act were caught. I had to see them. I had to understand, to know why."

He heaved a great sigh.

"Sometimes there are no reasons to things. These men were terribly crass and cruel, conscienceless. They stole to survive. They killed if they felt like it. They raped if they felt like it. Of course they were sentenced to death. But that was not good enough for me. I wanted a part in it. Insane with grief, I made a very bad decision. One I am living with and will live with for the rest of my life. As I said, I had wealth and privilege. I knew people at the palace. I paid a dungeon guard a nice sum of money to let me in to where they were held, and others who knew me looked the other way.

"The guard had put them together in one chamber, and tied them to two wooden chairs. I told him to close the door and come back in an hour."

Doc closed his eyes, the blond lashes dark with moisture. Tears rolled down his cheeks.

"The things I did to them I cannot and will not describe to this day. As a physician, I knew what I was doing, and how to elicit the most pain before they--expired."

Snow realized his own eyes were wide, mesmerized at listening to this story.

"I grieved alone for two years in my home, barely eating, avoiding past friends. The locals surmised I had killed the two prisoners, but no one came for me. No one said a word to me. I went out only for food, and only occasionally. But one day I heard about the queen coming to power and the atrocities that followed in the White Hills. I thought with my skills I might find more bad men, and I could express my untold grief upon them.

"Instead, I found more victims than anything. I found Bash near to death and realized I could help him. Something dark lifted from me while I was nursing him back to life. I started to care again. Care for him. My heart opened when I thought it had died."

Now Doc reached for Bash, who sat beside him as close as Sleepy was to Snow. Bash met his hand and they clasped, fingers weaving together.

They became lovers, Snow thought to himself. Amid dark tragedy, life still tried to wrangle itself a home, a kinship.

"When Bash got well, we decided to stay together, make a life for ourselves. We found this little, mostly hidden cave. And all the rest fell into place over the past ten years. Hap came next. Then Grump and Sneezy together. Sleepy. Dope. I have used these hands only for

104

good since finding Bash. I have never harmed, but I will live with the memory of my past deeds for the rest of my life."

A silence followed the circle of stories. Everyone sat with their own thoughts. Finally, Hap got up and rummaged in a cupboard. He came up with more rum. It seemed they never ran out.

"Time for this now. Time for better stories, and more loving thoughts." He passed the bottle around.

Snow took a deep drink, and his shock at the men's tragedies slowly began to ease inside him.

"Now is all that counts," Doc said. "We can become prisoners to our pasts, but what does that get us? It may seem dark with no way out, maybe for a very long time. But if we can heal, if we can learn to hope again, we can laugh again. We can love."

All the men nodded.

"We are more than what has happened to us," Doc added.

A second time the rum was passed around until smiles replaced frowns and heavy hearts lifted in the shared affection of mutual support and brotherhood.

"It was necessary to share with you, Snow, and you with us. The sharing of stories binds us," Doc said.

Snow nodded. No one had yet to give their true names. Only Snow still had his name.

More rum made the rounds. The atmosphere, somber and weighted, slowly lightened.

"I need a nickname like yours," Snow said, after his third drink.

Sleepy leaned back, arms crossed. "I was thinking about that. How about Charming, as that is how I find you."

Grump snorted. "Woe. He's full of it."

Bash said, "Friday. That's when we found him."

"We found him on a Saturday!" argued Dope.

"Puck," said Hap. "He's quite sprite-like."

"Quartz for his hair," Sneezy offered.

"Well? What do you think?" Doc asked Snow.

"You all have been thinking about this before now?"

"Yes." It was said in unison.

"Your names all honor me. But I think—hmm." He leaned his chin on his up-turned palm. "Maybe Quartz fits?"

Grump shook his head. "Why does he get to pick? I didn't!"

Hap laughed. "Grump, yours just fits. We can't stop calling you that."

"Quartz it is," said Doc.

Sleepy looked slightly disappointed that Charming did not win. But just the fact that he'd said aloud that Snow was charming was enough to make Snow's blood sing.

"More rum!" Hap said.

The atmosphere turned to one of comfort and soft gleaming light.

Sneezy brought out the cards. Doc retired to his chair and his knitting. Bash sat at his feet, reading.

The cat walked back and forth before the hearth, tail swishing.

Now it made sense to Snow why Bash stayed so close to Doc. Maybe all the men shared love with one another, but Bash and Doc were a couple. As were Grump and Sneezy.

Now Snow was one of them.

Sleepy, turned to him and took his hand. "Pleased to meet you, Quartz."

Chapter Fifteen

There might have been a wind outside. But Snow did not hear or care. For within him a whirlwind had captured his heart and would not let go.

A thousand years. An evening. It was all now for him.

Sleepy turned and turned them in his bed, under the furs, all naked muscle, skin, lips, springy cock. Pressing as much of their bodies together as they could, sliding, humping, trailing fire-kisses, Sleepy made Snow come, then spilled himself all over his hip.

They wrestled to the point of breathlessness.

Smiling wide in the darkness as Sleepy held him while they recovered, Snow whispered, "Sleepy, may I ask your real name?"

"Don't tell," he whispered back, kissing him like a warm breeze on his lips. "It's Benjamin."

"That's a beautiful name."

Sleepy gave a soft grunt, and turned himself and Snow until Snow lay on top of him, looking down at him in shadow.

Snow added, "A beautiful name for a beautiful man."

Sleepy ran his fingers all up and down Snow's back and ass. Big hands clutched his cheeks intimately, fingers delving lightly, possessively into his crack.

"You're the beautiful one," Sleepy breathed.

The caresses made circles, lines, zigzags, tingling his skin. Snow was young and eager. He stirred again, quick and ready before Sleepy could find his second wind.

Sleepy teased his ass for more minutes, making Snow squirm against him, then tipped him onto his side and burrowed under the covers to suck him.

Snow lay back as warm palms spread his thighs and a wet mouth found its target, first sucking at his balls, then his straining cock. The suction made his very soul quake.

Pine, autumn, dust, smoke. Sleepy smelled of deepness now, and heat, and Snow knew his lover's own arousal had returned. He gripped Sleepy's shoulders, digging in with the tips of his fingers.

That sturdy, sweet mouth went up and down his length, wet, hot, sucking as he pulled up, licking over the tip every time. Snow's mind spun. Maybe he should have been nicknamed Dizzy.

The ecstasy twirled him up and up to darkness, but nothing unfriendly. This dark offered pleasure upon pleasure for eternity. Nothing forgotten. Love undeterred.

The pressure on his cock sent weightless ebbs and flows of energy straight through his bones. He wanted to rise up and felt his hips thrust, unbidden. Forcing himself to remain still so Sleepy could regain a rhythm, Snow helplessly floated on his euphoria. He'd crested quickly the first time around, but this second time he could enjoy himself.

Sleepy grunted, taking him deep, swallowing around him. He was slick and the mouth moved freely over his skin, pushing, pulling, licking.

He could not get enough of Sleepy.

His heavy breathing filled the room and the men in the back bedroom had to be hearing it. He cared at first. Trying to hold his breath. Be silent. Then he didn't care at all as Sleepy went slowly over his tip, laving with his tongue, licking and licking. Sucking lightly as one hand milked the base of his shaft.

Nothing had ever felt like this. Nothing.

Down his lover went again, drawing him in deep, then sucking up. A little more of that and he would fly away to pieces.

Snow let out a small groan. Felt his balls tighten. Sleepy felt it too, caressing them with his palm, bobbing faster. Three more times and everything went white. His cock pulsed and pulsed, wringing itself dry.

Sleepy held him stilled in his mouth for a long time, warm and comforting. After a while, his cock slid from wet and heat. Sleepy trailed damp kisses up his abdomen, stomach, ribs and chest. Then he kissed Snow on the lips, mouth open, devouring. He tasted the tart excitement of himself. The thick cream.

Snow wrapped his arms and legs around him, feeling Sleepy's hard cock trail up his inner thigh.

When the long kiss finally ended, Snow said, "You are amazing."

Sleepy's grin spread across Snow's cheek as he left more kisses there and along his temple and into his hair.

108

Snow said, clinging, "I want to taste you, too."

Sleepy pulled himself up along Snow's body until he straddled his chest. He was bare to the cold now but seemed not to feel it.

Snow's head was propped with pillows, and now he had the perfect view in the dimness of a gorgeous cock.

Sleepy took hold of it in one hand and pointed it toward Snow's mouth.

Snow opened, sticking out his tongue, and lightly licked the revealed shining head as Sleepy's fingers pulled back the foreskin.

Sleepy groaned.

Snow grabbed his hips and pulled at him for more.

Gently, Sleepy painted Snow's lips with the tip of his cock before placing it at the entrance to Snow's mouth and slowly pushing in.

Snow accepted him with growing excitement, sucking the head. Taste of salt. And tart pre-come. And the sweetness of Sleepy. Of Benjamin. His love.

Already he was addicted.

With slow reverence, and a credit to his disciplined fortitude to not rush Snow, Sleepy pushed his cock in and out of Snow's mouth. Like a polite introduction. A tribute of himself. Making sure he was giving a gift and not taking more than what was offered.

Snow could not have asked for a more sensitive lover.

He loved the act. For his first time taking a man into his mouth he was, for a second, afraid of fumbling. But he remembered how it had felt when Sleepy sucked him that morning and then again only moments ago, and thought about that pleasure as he taught himself to reciprocate.

The stiff cock was smooth and delightful, strong and powerful, but waiting. Ready to burst only when Snow was ready to take it all.

He licked about the ridge and tongued the underside as he felt the head rub against the roof of his mouth. He remembered how prettily pink that tip was when it had peeked at him more than once, how long the shaft got in full arousal, smooth and perfect, decorated with two visible jagged lines of veins.

Even from afar, he'd studied that cock. He'd been embarrassed at himself at first.

Not anymore.

Minding his teeth, he sucked harder, pressing his lips inward, wagging his tongue. Sleepy gave a strained groan.

Yes, that was it. Snow took one hand from Sleepy's hip and cupped his balls, a gentle massage.

Warm liquid filled his mouth and he realized Sleepy was silently coming, breath held, leg muscles tightening about his ribs. Snow swallowed the pungent essence, suckling for more, hungry for more. The cock pulsed and he felt additional spurts coat the back of his throat. He swallowed faster.

When Sleepy pulled out, he raised himself over Snow. "Oh my, oh my" he kept whispering, and pressed his lips to Snow's.

They turned in the bed and lay side to side, facing each other, legs entangled.

Clinging front to front, they kissed themselves to sleep.

*

They slept heavily, only to wake at dawn and do it all over again.

Snow came twice in quick succession.

"Is this normal?" he gasped, trying to keep his whisper soft.

Sleepy was able to whisper back now that he didn't have a cock in his mouth. "New lovers are this way. Insatiable. But long-time lovers, too. When I first came to live here, we couldn't get Grump and Sneezy out of bed sometimes. On weekends they'd fuck all day. And they've known each other since childhood."

Snow chuckled at the statement and the crude but sweet context of the word *fuck*. Grump used the word often, but he'd never heard Sleepy say it. Until now.

They curled up together and dozed. Once, Sleepy got up and brought them both cool mugs of water. Snow did not realize how parched he was until he drank the entire contents.

Grateful to have such a considerate lover, he thanked him with another blowjob.

They slept late and Snow woke giggling, something he hadn't done since he was a child.

Sleepy laughed and peppered him with kisses all over. Then complimented his skin, his hair, his lips and eyes, his cock. He said, "You are the loveliest person I've ever seen, man or woman. So handsome. So alluring. I wish they would have let me call you Charming."

"You can secretly call me that in bed," Snow suggested with a sly smile.

"Oh, I will. I will."

Snow hugged him then, hard and strong as if he never wanted to let him go.

Eventually, hunger forced them from their bed.

Dope was already up and cooking, pretending to ignore them. But he threw them a few wide grins as they washed and got dressed in front of the fire.

"I feel like I should bow before you," Dope murmured.

"No," said Snow. "Never feel that way. I mean it."

Dope turned away, mumbling under his breath.

Soon, the others joined them. Everyone smiled. Even Grump.

Later, the chores began. Snow offered to help.

Grump made a face at him. "I'll show you how to do the laundry."

"Yes!" Snow wanted to help.

Laughter followed them toward the back room.

Snow heard someone, possibly Doc, say, "I've never heard of anyone so eager to do laundry."

"Oh," said another voice that sounded like Hap. "He's in love. Everything is fun when you're in love."

Grump was a patient teacher, and soon they had heated pails of water and two washboards between them, and were hanging clothing, sheets and cleaning rags to dry all over the back bedroom. Laundry for seven men and a household took a long time. But Snow loved every moment of it.

When they finished, the room looked like a tent more than a cave.

That afternoon, Bash and Dope taught Snow how to make miner's stew. And bread. They taught him how to knead the dough and set it aside to rise, then later how to wrap it in oilcloth and place the loaf deep in the embers to bake.

"One day," Doc commented, "we really ought to haul a stove up here."

The others all grunted in accord.

When Sneezy and Hap prepared to go out and fill pails with snow, since seven—now eight—men used up a lot of water, Snow wanted to go with them.

"He's Quartz now. One of us. He can come," Hap said.

Sleepy decided to accompany him, ever the protective boyfriend.

Snow wore his knit cap and red cloak. He bundled up his feet to better fit his borrowed boots and out they went into the fresh air.

Immediately, the blue sky seemed to lift him up. The floral scent of new flowers and budding grass swept over him. A cool breeze caressed his face.

They each took two pails and started along the path in the darker shadows of the woods to find fresh, un-melted snow.

Sleepy spoke. "In the summer months when the snow is mostly gone, we get water from a stream through the woods behind our home. Folks call it Leafbrook. It's not too far, but the snow right now is closer. I'll show the stream to you later."

"I'd like that," Snow said.

The four of them walked into the buzzing forest, watching squirrels scamper up rich, brown tree trunks, ducking as birds flitted from tree branch to tree branch singing to each other and gathering twigs for nests, or hunting the damp ground for worms.

They found snow mounds still untouched by the sun, pure white crystals of fresh water that when melted would be great for either cooking or washing.

They filled their pails and made their way back.

Dope stood by the little wooden door with eight more empty pails at his feet. He was puffing on a tiny pipe and blue curls of smoke rose up into the air.

"Figured we should stock up." He kicked one of the pails.

They set their full pails down and took the new ones, all going back into the sweetly scented, lively forest.

Snow glanced over his shoulder and saw Doc and Bash come to the entrance to help Dope gather up the full pails and take them indoors.

While they filled more pails, Snow was again entranced by the beauty surrounding him. And more grateful than ever for these seven wonderful men who had found him and brought him here.

After they returned with the extra pails of snow, Sleepy drew Snow aside.

"I can show you Leafbrook now, if you like."

Doc happened to be standing in the entryway, his glasses white with daylight.

Sleepy looked up at him, as if looking to a father for permission.

"I think it should be all right. Quartz is steady on his feet now."

"I feel fine. My feet still have pins and needles, but so much less. It helps to walk."

Doc nodded at him. "And the boots?"

"I stuffed more rags in the toes and they fit much better."

"Sleepy," Doc said softly. "Don't be long."

"We won't."

Hand in hand, Snow and Sleepy set out in the other direction behind their underground home. Sleepy's palm was warm and soft against his own, and his fingers wove with Snow's in such an affectionate and intimate gesture that Snow felt none of the chill in the mountain air, only warmth. Only the fulfillment of encompassing love.

Light slanted through the trees in misting rays. The new leaves sparkled green and white. Flowers of every color pushed through thin cracks in the snow.

Mud clung to their boots as they strived to find little paths of harder ground.

His heart full and the world brimming in such lush splendor, Snow would follow Sleepy anywhere.

The brook was a narrow ribbon of silver liquid light rushing through a gully of moss-covered rocks, low-hanging tree branches, and piles of old, dappled leaves.

It made a laughing sound.

Up ahead, something large moved. Snow jerked in startlement.

Sleepy put a hand on the back of his shoulder and pointed.

Upstream, a heron stood, knee-deep in tiny whitewaters, fishing for his meal. He was cloud-white and tall as a child with a long, graceful beak. A stunning creature of natural elegance.

"Oh." Snow could not remain silent at the sight.

"If I could, I'd do everything in my power to see you free like this all the time, with the worries of the world far away." Sleepy's voice was like a low wind-hum.

Snow turned his face up to him. "You already are."

Sleepy's head dipped. Snow pushed himself up on his toes. They kissed.

Their arms went around each other, Snow's up and over the broad shoulders, Sleepy's curved about his waist, hands pressed to the small of his back.

Snow ran his fingers up into Sleepy's hair as their kiss deepened. And how he wanted more right then. Starved for the cloying taste of him. Fire and ice. Earth and wind. A wild and gentle love at the same time but free and open. He wanted Sleepy to have him in the rough-hewn beauty that surrounded him, right here by the brook that chuckled and burbled with no agenda but its own purpose.

That was what this love felt like. Something that had its own purpose separate from all things that preyed upon them, worries, strife and fate and tragic pasts.

It was so lovely that these men found each other. That they had found Snow.

And Doc, such a true healer. Could their combined energy cure a blighted land held in thrall by an evil ruler?

He did not know. Only this was real now. This kiss. Deepening into a sort of sweet-raw, fight-submit, longing hunger.

It was the loneliest, most vulnerable feeling to fall in love. And the best thing that could ever have happened to him.

Snow groaned, wanting to merge their bodies, wanting—he could not even define it!

Sleepy pulled back from the kiss and nearly lifted him off his feet, the tips of Snow's boots barely touching the damp soil of the riverbank. He laughed right in Snow's face, eyes sparkling. Their noses rubbed.

"I want you," Snow said.

"My crystal Quartz, my rare flower. Such a gift you are."

Snow scowled at the poetic phrasing. "Does that mean you want me?" He scrunched his lips together, making a face.

"Always."

"You can have me. Right here."

Sleepy started to shake his head. "You'll catch a chill again."

"No. I'm hot. Feverish. All over. You can wrap me up in this cloak, take everything else off—"

Sleepy did not need to be told twice. His strong arms picked Snow up until he lay against his chest, then walked them both to a carpet of soft spongy grass by a low-branched tree and set him upon it.

Snow laughed all the way, clinging to his shoulders. He loved this big man so much.

The brook chattered. Birds sang. There would be musical accompaniment to their lovemaking today.

Sleepy leaned over him and began undoing the buttons of his shirt and trousers, pushing aside his clothing. He pushed Snow's trousers all the way to the tops of his boots, then said, "I won't remove the boots. I won't leave your feet unprotected."

"Fine," Snow agreed. It was arousing this way, half-clothed, legs trapped, his pale, slender body laid back on the red cloak's off-white wool lining like an offering.

"Now you," Snow commanded.

Sleepy frowned a question.

"Your shirt. Take it off."

Sleepy complied, his pecs gleaming in the natural light, brown nipples hard. His shoulders rippled, his arms flexed as he folded his white muslin shirt and set it on top of Snow's.

Snow could not take his eyes off the perfect body before him. Hard, brown skin tight and fit, waist narrowing beneath ribs, stomach flat and showing ripples of muscle. When the trousers were lowered, that lovely cock sprang free, glistening at the pink tip all pretty and wanting him.

Snow grinned up at Sleepy, who answered by covering him with kisses and caresses all over, pushing his legs apart, hands going underneath to his buttocks and lifting him up until he could take his hard cock into his mouth. No preamble, just a downward motion, and a long, hard suck.

Snow's head tipped back, eyes rolling up in pleasure. He shivered.

Sleepy must have thought he was cold and blindly sought the edge of the cloak and covered his chest with it.

But Snow was far from cold. His body was flame. His mind ablaze.

He opened his eyes to the blue sky framed by dark, new-leafed branches. Lost himself in the depthless void. But all the time he knew he was not alone, for Sleepy held him, caressed him, loved him. He drank Snow's pleasure until Snow's flight ended and he fell gracefully, like a feather, back to Earth.

He turned and made Sleepy lie next to him, then returned the pleasure, covering them both with his cloak, making a tent.

Beneath the folds of warm wool, he caressed Sleepy's achingly handsome body, leaving trails of kisses everywhere. He held the proud cock in his fist and worked it, licking and sucking at the same time.

He sought the white nectar, the fountain of ecstasy, and Sleepy did not disappoint.

After, they lay curled together under the cloak. They kissed some more but dared not doze or sleep.

"We should get back," Sleepy said.

Snow clutched him tight, moaning in protest. He loved the wildness of this place, the impulsive expressions of their love.

"Is something wrong with me that I always want more?" Snow asked.

"No." Sleepy yawned.

"I want you to touch me everywhere. All the time," Snow said like a petulant child.

"I want that, too."

"I'm not usually such a brat. But I want more. More."

"There is a way men also join—" Sleepy stopped, cleared his throat.

Snow turned his head, raising one eyebrow. "Yes?"

Sleepy nodded.

"You'll show me?"

Sleepy grinned. "Maybe. Maybe some time. But we must go." Abruptly, he sat up, his back muscles flexing, the skin like satin as Snow reached up to trace a line down his spine.

He helped Snow pull up his trousers, then handed him his shirt.

All the while, Snow could not stop thinking about what Sleepy had just said. How did men join together further? There was only one way he could think, and of course now it all made sense when he'd heard servants or the rougher sorts of guards curse each other with the term *ass-bugger*.

But it never dawned on him it was a real thing for pleasure, only for degrading remarks, the guards acting as if a person of that sort was beneath them in stature.

116

He shuddered to think of the act, but still wondered. If Sleepy mentioned it, then men must do it and feel pleasure, or why bother? But it had to hurt, too. It had to.

When he finished buttoning everything up, Sleepy stood. He reached down and pulled Snow to his feet.

Snow lay his palm flat against Sleepy's cheek, feeling a roughness of hair. Every morning Sleepy shaved when he washed. But his hair grew fast and by evening shadowed his face. Snow thought he looked even more handsome that way. Like he did now with the faint hint of his dark beard.

"What?" Sleepy tilted his head.

"You."

"Me what?"

"Just." Snow shook his head until his knit cap loosened. "Everything."

Sleepy smiled and reached to push Snow's hair more securely under his cap and straighten it. "Ready?"

Snow nodded.

Sleepy took his hand.

Chapter Sixteen

They had argued. Not about anything serious.

Sleepy had wanted to stay home from work to be with Snow.

Snow assured him he'd be fine. He'd spent all the past week alone while the men worked and he'd been sick then. Now he was well.

"You just want to fool around instead of work, Sleepy," Grump commented.

Sleepy glared at him.

"I'll do all the chores," Snow said. "Then when you all get home from work, you can relax."

Doc reminded Snow. "No going out for any reason. Do you understand that?"

"Very clearly." Snow was still scared by what he thought he'd seen in the woods. Although he'd talked himself into believing it was indeed an afterimage from the sun.

Sleepy acquiesced, but said, "I don't want you doing all the work while we're gone, not all by yourself."

Dope nodded. "I agree."

Sneezy said, "It seems wrong for a prince to be doing our chores."

Snow stepped forward. "I want to do the work. And besides," he smirked. "If I'm alone all day, none of you will be here to stop me. So you'd best leave a list of things you want done."

And that was how Snow found himself dusting the shelves and cupboards, wiping down the big and small tables, and sweeping the bricks in front of the hearth. Then he shook out all the blankets from all seven beds and remade them. The linens were all right, having been washed on Sunday by himself and Grump.

He liked having something to do and even better, he felt he was contributing to the group.

When suppertime came round, the place was looking good. He'd stacked the empty water pails. He'd done the dishes. He'd put them away where they belonged just as he'd been shown. He'd neatened all the clothing on hooks, folded what had been tossed on beds and chairs and left them in neat stacks on the beds.

After he ate a lunch of fresh bread and butter, and salty cheese, he was refreshed. It wasn't time yet to prepare the evening meal—he'd be making miner's stew—so he rummaged about for more things to do. He checked the water closet, but Dope had cleaned it top to bottom just yesterday and it still looked fresh.

Curious, he went to Sleepy's trunk at the end of his bed. He'd seen Sleepy take clothing from it, and the red cloak he'd given him. But he'd never really looked inside.

He put his hand on the top, fingers under the edge to open, then stopped. Was he intruding into a man's personal space? After everything they'd shared, Snow thought not. But still, he felt funny to look at a man's belongings that were put away in a closed box without that man present. It was like spying.

He walked about the home, petted the cat, and thought about other things. For a while, he read one of Bash's books by the fire, his feet up.

Then it was time to start the meal. He prepared all the ingredients. He built up the fire.

Then everything was done. The men had not yet come home. He could tell by how much the candles had burned that there was still more time before they arrived.

Again, he went to Sleepy's chest.

Taking a deep breath, he opened it.

On top lay three neatly-folded shirts and three pairs of trousers. He also had several pairs of knit socks rolled into balls. And a white nightshirt. Sleepy wore no undergarments, so Snow was not surprised to find there were none in the chest. There was a tattered children's book of illustrated fairytales. Something he must have loved as a child and saved from his past. Also, two balled up knitted scarves, quite worn at the edges, one red, one blue.

But there was more beneath this stuff. Guilt rippled through Snow as he rummaged down. He heard the rattle of metal on metal. His hand touched something smooth and long. Cold steel.

Pushing back the soft garments, Snow saw by candlelight a collection of knives and swords. Weapons.

So many. He sat back, letting the wood lid close.

He had not counted, but there were maybe half a dozen sheathed knives, and at least three swords. Not broadswords, but smaller.

Many men had weapons. Of course they did. But so many?

Scratching his head, Snow went to stir the stew.

Then he found himself standing before the big bedroom and eying the other chests of all the other men.

Before he realized that he could be seen as a trespasser, or worse, he'd gone through all of them.

Each chest held just as many weapons as Sleepy's, some more. Each man had more knives and swords than any one man could wear at a time. And they were not displayed; they were hidden.

But why?

These man had secrets. He knew that. Just as Snow had had his own secrets. They'd shared them. Snow knew they were part of a resistance. But they had said they were not organized. But Snow began to wonder if they had more going on than they had admitted when everyone was revealing their truths. He began to see events of the last week and a half in a new light.

Snow had been taken from his tower prison in the middle of a dark and cold night. He'd been accompanied by guards and the huntsman. When he refused to walk any further barefoot in the cold snow, a guard slung him over his shoulder and they all took him far into the hills. Why the hills?

No one but the old lady knew about this, obviously, or he wouldn't have been grabbed while sleeping and while it was still the deep of night.

How could he have been rescued by these seven beautiful men just happening to be nearby?

It didn't make sense. The men had a routine. Work. Home. Sleep.

What were they doing out in the middle of the night? In the cold? Why had the guards vanished leaving the huntsman alone to finish his job of killing Snow?

Too many questions.

His mind tangled up in all the details. Were they hiding other things from him? Did they not fully trust him? Or was it because he was the prince?

They had always known who he was. He had found that out but then thought nothing of it. His secret had not been so secret after all. But he figured it didn't take a genius to put together his name, the color of his hair, and his age. And of course he spoke with a fine, educated accent. His hands and skin were soft. He'd never done rough work.

He was a rich boy, upper class. An aristocrat.

But his findings led him to believe now it was more than these men simply knowing who he was. Was his escape planned from the very beginning?

In truth, Doc had been honest with him to a point. He had said they had underground connections with people, factions who wanted an end to the queen's rule. Plus, Doc said he had once had friends at the palace.

But how far did this go?

Snow waited at the table, head on his folded hands, for the men to come home.

The stew smelled good. He had fresh bread warming.

He wanted to know more. But if he confronted them at dinner, he would be confessing to snooping in their private things. The thought terrified him probably more than it should, but all his life after his mother died, he'd been ignored or outright rejected. He knew these men weren't like the old lady or the people she had working for her, but his fears remained.

He would not tell. Confronting the men, at least right now, was out of the question.

He heard the footsteps coming up the frosty path outside the little wooden door.

Snow's heartbeat increased. He knew it was them. All seven of them. And that they revered and protected him. They had always known he was the prince.

Still, his nerves jangled and there was a low buzzing in his head.

Sleepy came down the passage first. He went to Snow and put his arms around his shoulders, kissing the top of his head. "Mmm, smells good in here. I'm hungry!"

Snow ducked his head, holding back a grin.

The others soon followed, making noise, talking excitedly.

All made comments about how clean the place was. And about how good dinner smelled.

Soon they were all seated around the table with bowls of Snow's first home-cooked meal.

Only then did Snow's heart calm and his mind quiet. Everything was normal again. The warmth. The brotherhood. The love.

Snow was where he belonged. Safe. Cared for.

Everyone had second helpings of the stew.

Grump and Sneezy insisted on cleaning up afterward, since Snow had done all the cooking. But Snow would not allow it.

"You worked all day, too," he told them.

But they all helped him. Dope dried the cleaned dishes with a cloth and put them away.

Soon they were enjoying the evening, relaxing, playing games, reading, knitting. Nothing out of the ordinary. It was hard for Snow to imagine these men sneaking out in the night to participate in secret plans, one of which included rescuing a prince.

But then again, as he gazed upon them all around the table and the hearth, it didn't seem so far-fetched. They were young—Doc being the oldest did not look past forty—and strong and smart. They were organized and they had a pact of trust that could not be unbroken.

But if it was the truth that they had secret midnight missions in defiance of the queen, why did they keep that detail from him?

The simple answer was they could not yet completely trust him.

A voice mumbled and he heard the word "Snow."

He looked up from his cards, blinking.

"You're quiet tonight." Sleepy gazed at him with soft, dark eyes.

"I am?"

He nodded and so did Hap.

"Everything all right today? Nothing strange happened, did it?"

"No. It was quiet and wonderful, actually. I loved keeping the house for you all."

"Tired?" Sleepy asked.

Snow wasn't but he shrugged.

They played cards and the men talked about ordinary things. Work. Which consisted of splitting rocks, lifting rocks and hauling

122

rocks. The weather. Which was quite beautiful in May here in the mountains. And food. Which mostly was about what they might have for meals every day this week. It was important to plan ahead, Hap said, because if they ran short of certain items, he was the runner to Hans' farm for extra supplies. And sometimes he and Dope took an afternoon off and went to the nearest village.

Organized. These men were impeccable to a T.

They were capable of many great things. Healing. Building. Empathy for less fortunate souls. Forming trusting groups. Keeping pacts. Certainly, they were capable of planning the rescue of one unlucky prince.

Again, Snow glanced around the table, and at Doc on his chair and Bash leaning against his knee. Knitting. Reading. Ordinary men. Yes. But also, extraordinary.

They were his heroes. And one day Snow would repay them as they deserved. He could find a way. One day.

Chapter Seventeen

Snow rolled away from Sleepy's warm, hard body and lay panting on his back.

Sleepy made him feel things he'd never experienced.

How he loved him.

The week had passed in peace. Snow enjoyed keeping the house. He never again peeked into the men's private things, and never mentioned what he'd found to any of them.

He was especially excited for today. It was Friday. That meant he could spend the whole weekend with Sleepy. They could be together and, he hoped, go outside again. Go for a few walks. For Snow was feeling quite cooped up. He'd been living far too long in closed in environments. He craved the fresh air and beauty of nature.

Also, he felt safe here in the higher elevations. The chance of anyone seeing him, let alone recognizing him especially if he wore his cap, was slim.

Snow stretched under the furs, watching the shadows on the rocky walls weave and dance in the dimness. The hearth was mostly embers. Someone would have to get up and stir it, sweep out the ash, put on fresh wood. Cords of chopped wood lined the wall by the front entrance.

Snow would do it. But in a minute. He was still coming down from the euphoria Sleepy brought him. Still basking.

Sleepy turned to him in the darkness, placing two kisses on his forehead and temple.

Snow reached up and ran his hand along his bicep, back and forth. The skin was smooth as silk.

They did not need words to communicate their love.

Soft, hushed breaths came from the other room. Partners loving each other. Snow imagined no one was left out.

He lay dozing, dreaming for long minutes. Sleepy lay breathing into his ear.

Snow dreamed a gathering upon the snow. Lights were strung everywhere, lanterns and oil lamps dangling from the trees. Music played. A zither. A flute. A lyre.

In the dream, Sleepy laughed and kissed him on the lips. He had a garland of white flowers in his dark brown hair.

Snow eased from the dream and opened his eyes. He got up, put on the red cloak and nothing else, then went to tend the fire and put the first pail of water on to heat for the men's bathing.

*

He had keen eyes that had grown used to the dark. As Snow passed by the back bedroom to the water closet, he saw things. Nearly every morning now. The men were less shy now that he'd taken Sleepy as a lover.

He saw two to a bed. Sometimes three if activity was high. This meant to him couples invited thirds into their beds.

He would try to hurry by and get his business done and return to the front room to start to set the table. But sometimes he lingered by the side of the water closet, out of sight.

He saw things.

Outlines of beautiful bodies, muscular silhouettes. Kneeling. Lying back. Sometimes standing while another knelt at his feet.

They made love right out in the open. With each other. Or watching each other.

There was touching, caressing, sucking. But there was more. The thing Sleepy had mentioned. About men connecting in another way. Truly joining.

A man might be on his hands and knees with a second standing or kneeling from behind. One naked, backside exposed, spread. And the other thrusting in and out. A third might join, pressing himself against the kneeling man's face to be suckled.

Snow was fascinated. He heard their sounds of pleasure. And the slick thrusts, like noisy, bodily kisses. Wet. Oiled up.

It made him turned on to watch, but also shy. Then he'd scurry by and into the orange light of the front room where he and Sleepy would wash each other with loving attention.

Snow learned a lot over the next weeks. How to make meals. The art of dusting. Cleaning. Laundry. Bed-making. And sex.

He loved to watch. One time Hap, who was thrusting against Dope from behind, saw him watching and beckoned him with an upturned hand and a lofty grin.

Snow was hard and naked behind his red cloak. But he declined, hurrying back to Sleepy's arms all warm and comforting and known.

He guessed he was just too shy. And too enamored with Sleepy.

Sleepy was his love. He wanted Sleepy more than anything. All the time. But he could not deny that the other men, all beautiful in their own ways, did not mesmerize him. Little spy that he was.

Softly, while they lay in bed, Snow asked Sleepy, "Do you miss them?"

"What?"

"The others."

"They have not gone away."

"Yes, but what I mean is, do you miss being with them. Sharing like they do. With each other." He paused, biting his lower lip. "Sexually."

"What makes you think—"

"I know you all shared everything before I came. But then you devoted yourself to me. And I love you for it. More than ever. But I just wondered."

Sleepy pulled him close. "You are the best. I've never felt anything like I do when I'm with you. The others understand. Doc encouraged me."

"But this is your family. Your lovers."

"I love them. But I am *in love* with you."

Snow had so many questions. He wanted to know more. Everything. Had Sleepy been with them all, or was he circumspect in his bed partners?

"It's amazing what you all have."

"Yes. It is." Sleepy kissed him. "We are all special. And we are all lucky we found each other."

"You saved each other."

Sleepy nodded against his cheek.

"And me," Snow added.

Sleepy gave another nod, his nose pressing into Snow's hair.

"Did you plan it?" Snow shut his mouth. Closed his eyes. Had he gone too far?

Softly. "You know what happened that night."

"I was frozen. Nearly comatose."

126

"The huntsman had a knife. He pressed it to your chest."

"Yes." Snow could still feel it, the sharp tip scratching through the thin cotton of his old, worn shirt. The only shirt he'd owned for two years. There was little doubt in his mind the huntsman wanted to kill him. But the guards who had accompanied them, and then suddenly vanished? Who were they? And why did they not stay to see the execution through?

The conversation ended there. But later that day, Snow saw Sleepy talking in whispers to Doc. Snow pretended not to see them as he wiped down the big table. But in his side-vision, he saw them glance his way and knew. They were discussing him. And it could only be about what he'd said to Sleepy that morning in the privacy of their bed.

For the next few days, Snow was of mixed thoughts about his conviction that these men had been involved in planning his rescue. Of course he was happy they had saved his life. But at the same time, he did not want to be responsible for anyone getting hurt or killed on his behalf.

Yes, people lived and died for their kings and queens, their princes and princesses, but Snow might never gain his proper inheritance. In that case, he was just an ordinary citizen. No one special. In fact, he liked that thought very much.

But if he could do anything to help a realm in the midst of cruel law, hard times and a mad queen, the responsible thing to do would be to use his title and do some good.

To save them in return. That would be his own private mission. He wanted his new family protected. If it came down to that, he would give his life to make it so.

Chapter Eighteen

Summer came upon the land. There were really only two seasons up in the hills. Winter and summer. Winter could last as long as eight or nine months some years. They were lucky if summer lasted from June through September. Even then, freak snowstorms came and went.

Every day, the men left for work and Snow stayed behind to keep the hearth and home. Doc would remind him often to never to go outside without one of the men beside him.

Usually Snow had ample supplies. But if he needed extra water for cooking and had used up all the drip-collection pots, he would have to wait until the men came home to fetch it for him or accompany him to Leafbrook. If he wanted fresh flowers for the table, he would have to wait. If he became overwhelmed with the desire for fresh air, he would have to quench his craving. He was told that if he was alone, he was never to open the small wooden front door. Not even a crack.

His paranoia made it easy for him to obey. But his feeling of imprisonment, of being held back his whole life, made it difficult.

But every day he bided his time. He made their home neat and shining. He learned to make variations of stews, soups and casseroles. He learned to make muffins, cookies and even cakes if he had the correct ingredients.

The men joked. "Quartz is going to make us fat!" They loved him more every day and Snow felt an acceptance like nothing he'd ever had in his life; it made his spirit soar.

A week before, Snow had folded and placed aside on a wide shelf in the bedroom, all the furs. The weather had changed. The days grew warmer, though the cave retained a cool air if Snow allowed the hearth fire to wane. Single blankets were enough to keep the men warm during the shorter summer nights, and they often shared beds with each other, so the furs were quite unnecessary.

In the early mornings, and the evenings, Snow was allowed, if accompanied, outside for brief walks, but dawn and dusk were all he saw. The shadowing hills. An orange and pink sky. Dying or awakening night breezes lifting the locks of his hair that had escaped from his knit cap. On weekends only, he saw what he missed. The sun glittering on the brook. The leaves flashing. The color green so verdant it threatened to blind.

The more he saw of the outdoors, the more he wanted to be free to be in it whenever he wanted. Would this gloom he had hanging over him his whole life ever leave?

Sil jumped up on a chair by the table, then walked daintily across his freshly wiped tabletop.

"You'll leave footprints," Snow gently reprimanded.

Haughty, she ignored him. The promptly threw up a hair ball.

"I used the last of the clean water to wash that down!" He used a dirty rag and wiped the hairball away.

Sil sat, undeterred, and lifted her paw, biting at an extended claw.

Snow had some drinking water left for himself. But not enough for all the men. They'd be extra thirsty on a hot summer day. And then they'd have to wait. One or two would have to accompany him to the brook for more water. Being helpful, they'd all take pails to help. But after a day's work, they should not have to.

He sat and watched the unconcerned cat and thought about how easy it would be to deftly make his way through the woods to the brook. He knew the private path now. He knew how to leave no footprints. How to walk in silence. How to listen and scent and feel the air for other presences. Sleepy, Hap and Sneezy had taught him these skills. Just in case.

It would be easy. So easy to just slip out for a minute. To get the water. The men would never know. They'd think they had stocked up enough water for the day.

Plus, the cat needed grass to settle her stomach. In winter, she did without, but now her supply in her box had wilted and turned brown. It would be nice for her to have fresh grass to nibble.

And besides, it was summer. So lovely out. He'd been cooped up for days. He longed to walk in the sun.

As if hearing his thoughts, Sil looked up from her bath on the clean table, her green eyes accusing.

"You wouldn't tell if I just slipped out for a minute, would you, Sil?" he whispered. "I won't go far."

She blinked.

He reached out and stroked her plush back. She stood and arched for him.

"All right then. It's settled."

Snow felt no fear. There was no one out there. There hadn't been anyone by, not even the farmer Hans except for that one time, since Snow had come to live here. He knew he'd be fine.

He felt Sil's eyes on him as he stood, donned his knit cap, and went to the stack of empty pails. He picked up two and turned to look at her. On the way to the river, he'd fill his pockets with grass.

"It's all right. I'll only be a minute."

Up the narrow entryway, Snow went.

Sil let out a small meow, unusual for her. She was mostly noncommittal.

At the entrance, Snow set down one pail, unlocked the door with a latch from the inside—from the outside one needed a key—and slowly pushed it open.

A brightness blinded him for a few seconds. But he knew the step forward was flat and a little down. He picked up the second pail and made his way into the day.

As he was shoving the door closed behind him, a silver streak of fur dashed past his booted feet.

"Sil!"

Only once had Sil accidentally gotten out in the weeks Snow had lived here. The men were careful about her since she was an indoor cat who stood no chance against wolves and bears.

She always came at Doc's call, responding instantly to his voice and was deposited back indoors within minutes.

But now Doc wasn't here.

"Sil," Snow said again, setting down his pails. "Come here, kitty. You need to stay inside."

Sil stretched and slowly walked toward the center of the path that led to the woods, sniffed a sprig of grass, then sat. She looked off into the forested distance.

Snow walked toward her. "Come on," he said quietly. "Come on, pretty. Let's go home."

Sil looked up at him calmly just as Snow was almost in reach, then darted from his grasp to the shadowed edge of the wood.

Sighing heavily, Snow glanced about.

For a summer day, the sky was overfull with clouds. One drifted against the sun and the shadows lengthened.

A breeze picked up and it wasn't quite warm. He had not worn his cloak. Thought he wouldn't need it.

"Sil, sweetie, come here."

The cat ignored him, having found some taller green grass to bite and chew. The others often brought fresh grass to Sil for her to eat. Doc said it was good for her digestion since she didn't get to be outdoors. In the summer they gathered catnip for her. It made sense she would go for the greens.

Slowly, Snow stalked her. He approached her from behind, preparing to snatch her into his arms, when again she pounced away, this time chasing a fly.

"Sil, please, kitty-kitty!" Impatient, he ran after her this time, only causing her to go more astray. There was a lot to distract a cat in the woods. Snapping leaves. Dangling twigs. Birds fluttering. Insects flitting. Butterflies lazing on the wind.

Before he knew it, he and Sil were deeper into the woods and off the path than he'd ever intended to go. But he had to get her. It would break Doc's heart if he lost his beloved cat. It would break all the men's hearts.

"Sil!"

She turned and gave him an indolent look. The sky had darkened a little more. She looked up, then back at him.

"Yes, I know, it's getting colder. You need to come home," he said to the cat.

Slowly, she walked toward him and purred, weaving herself between his legs.

Finally! "That's a good kitty." He reached down and picked her up. She made her body limp in his arms.

Now he looked about them, turning with Sil in his grasp, recognizing nothing.

"Oh, now look what you've done. You've gotten us lost."

Big trees bent their trunks and arms toward him, chattering with new leaves, but ominous, cold.

The weather had turned even darker since the short time he'd emerged from home. The air drew up in a wintry tang.

They often had these little winters in the midst of June, up here in the White Hills. The storms might come on fast, then leave the next day without a trace.

He turned back the way he thought they'd come. "It's all right," he said to Sil. "We've only strayed ten minutes at most. Home isn't far."

But the woods snapped and cracked as the breeze turned to a wind. It blew by his ear with a cold hand.

Looking closely at the ground, he recognized a copse of rosemary by the trunk of one tree, and knew he'd passed it once, so he headed in that direction.

Hoof beats sounded. Or maybe it was only the wind.

A shiver crawled down his back.

He thought he saw a large animal go by in the distance. Or maybe it was just the swinging of low branches.

He hurried along the direction he thought he'd come. Again, the hoof beats resounded, closer this time, but he saw nothing.

Finally, he came to a clearing of bluebells and buttercups, rosemary and violets, and briefly the sun came out from behind a cloud and brightened the land. He saw a road.

"Well, that's something, right, Sil? We're not completely lost."

Sil lay still in his arms, cooperative for the moment. But the hoof beats echoed again, closer, and before he could duck back into the shadows, a fancy white coach with gold trim came around a copse of trees and headed straight for him.

Four horses led the coach, plumed in tall white feathers, heads down. The road consisted of hard-packed mud, and very little dust rose.

Snow stood back with the cat, thinking maybe the coach would just pass and ignore him.

Instead, to his regret, it slowed. When it reached him, the driver, an indistinct figure in black sitting high up in the air, reined the big horses back and they stopped, snorting and pawing the hard-packed earth.

As soon as Snow saw the crest on the carriage, a snake and a dragon facing each other on a backdrop of blood-red, all rational thought plummeted into a dark abyss. He stopped breathing. He stood very still and stared straight ahead.

132

The side door to the carriage opened and a step folded outward and down.

The cat jumped from his arms and ran back into the trees.

A woman dressed all in ivory satins and white silks with her golden hair piled high and her white cloak lined with tiger fur falling about her slim, bare shoulders, stepped out. A dainty, jeweled slipper touched the ground, followed by another, until she stood in the road, a perfect image of royal excess.

Snow found himself face to face with the old lady.

"Hello, Snow." As if coming from deep in her chest, the voice held a cool, melodic tone, devoid of emotion.

This was it. He'd lost. He'd disobeyed Doc. He'd let everyone down. And now he knew he was about to die and no one would ever know what happened.

For a split second, he thought he might run. He judged he could out-run her, even with his cumbersome boots and imperfect feet, but the idea vanished as a dozen or more men on horseback appeared from the forest shadows and surrounded him. They were no one friendly. No one who wasn't in the charge of the queen.

Her pale blue eyes pierced him. "Poor boy, lost all this time. Aren't you happy to see me?"

He said nothing, frozen by her. Mind a jumble of terror.

"Kneel before me, boy!" She suddenly commanded.

When he didn't move, he heard a horse come up behind him, and the sound of a horse-whip weeping through the air. The leather hit him hard on the shoulder, and he fell to his knees in shock at the stinging impact.

She walked a slow circle about him. He tried to look up but she smacked at his face with a loose glove. "Head down!"

All he could see was white on white, her skirts, her glittery shoes, her pale be-ringed hands.

"Someone's been giving you aid and you will tell me who and maybe I will allow you to live."

He knew better. She could not allow him to live. Not after all this time. He might escape again. The continuation of his life threatened her power even more now.

"No one has helped me. I've been living most of this time in the streets of a village, stealing food."

"That is a lie." She stood before him now, her hands at her sides.

"It is not—" Before he could finish, she smacked him again, this time with her open hand.

Snowed rocked back on his knees. His feet dug into the ground, his freshly healed little toes starting to throb.

"It's simple, then. If you do not tell me the truth, I will have my men comb this forest and kill anyone who resides here. No one will question my orders when I tell them I have found the secret ring of rebels rumored to be hiding out here."

Shocked that she might know of the rebellion, and his friends' involvement, he remained silent. His mind clamoring for anything he could say to save his friends, his people, and the innocent lives of other farmers and forest dwellers in these upper elevations of the White Hills.

"Tell me," she commanded.

"There's been no one." A blast of wind washed over the tops of the trees, making them eerily creak.

"I can see you lie. Do you know how I know?"

He kept himself very still.

"You are wearing clean clothing. Your hands are clean. Your nails unbroken. You've had help. Do you take me for a fool?"

"No, Your Highness."

"I will have my men take you apart limb by limb, then. What do you say to that?"

Snow shut his eyes tight. For love, for family, he would not speak. "I surrender myself to you. For I have done nothing and no one has helped me. If I have offended you, I give my life to you willingly. Do as you please."

She gave disgusted little grunt. "You always were a problem. I should have done more than imprison you. I should have disposed of you the day your father died."

Snow's lungs shook. He could barely breathe. His worst nightmares were coming true. But the worst was not his death. No. It was the fact that he'd never see Sleepy again, hold him under the furs, love him. Sleepy would never know what happened to him. Sleepy would break into a million pieces. But maybe with Doc's healing and love, and the love of the others, he would be whole again. Snow could

134

only hope. For that one thing was more important to him than his own life.

He opened his eyes and looked up.

The old lady stepped back. For a moment, all Snow could hear was the wind whipping up as a summer storm came on. The birds had gone, and the insects. Even the little squirrels. He saw the forest turn evil. Leaves shuddered. Some fell and were thrashed upon the air, turning and turning.

The queen made a quick-snapped gesture with her hand and said, "Get up!"

Snow rose, unbalanced.

"Get in." She motioned to the carriage.

Snow looked inside. The seats were white leather, flawless. Pink and white silks hung against the windows. He stepped up into the carriage. The queen followed.

Inside the cabin, two leather-cushioned benches faced each other. She sat opposite him. A basket sat at her side, filled with bright red apples.

It was not the correct time of year for apples, but Snow did not question it.

She saw him eye the basket. "Ah, yes. I remember how much you used to love apples as a child. Are you hungry, perhaps?"

This was a tease. She would certainly not feed him if she was going to kill him.

He shook his head, though her memory was correct. He remembered the glory of Hans' apple pies when he'd first arrived at the cave. Hap had brought them home in a sack.

"I always carry a basket of apples with me. I love to feed the poor," she said.

Snow's eyebrows rose.

"Oh, does that surprise you? I am generous. I love my people."

Snow frowned.

"Snow, you and I have had some good times, haven't we, my dear?" She reached out and caressed his cheek. He tried not to recoil. "In the spirit of that, I will make a bargain with you."

Finding his voice, he said roughly, "What sort of bargain?"

The old lady's hand, now gloved again, reached into the basket and pulled out a shining red apple, the biggest of the lot.

"If you take this and eat it, I will let you go and never return here. I will not seek or harm your friends."

A trick, of course. Why would she give him food only to let him go? And why would he say no?

It made no sense. He rifled his memory for any solution. Anything about the queen and apples. And the poor. It hit him suddenly, like quick glance at a brief scene. He'd been fourteen or fifteen and overheard the servants gossiping.

One of them said, "The queen is nice. People say not, but she is."

The other replied, "How do you say that? She has people killed for no reason. My family is scared."

"She feeds the poor. That's quite a gesture of good will, isn't it?"

"Have you not heard the rumors? Every time she feeds the poor, illness follows. And death. Not all, but a lot more than normal. She's culling the poor, that's what they say in the village streets."

Snow gazed at her. Poisoned apples. That was how she did it. By helping the poor, she was really diminishing their ranks by tainting some of the food. Getting rid of what she called the vermin and trash of the land.

"Well?"

"I agree." Snow held out his hand. He knew she lied, but he had to hope she might leave as long as she knew he was dead. As long as he wasn't around to threaten her power play by his mere existence.

She placed the shiny apple in his palm. "Go ahead," she said. "It will do me well to see you eat. Then be off. Find your life. If you never bother me, I will never bother you. Or the friends you have in these mountains. How is that for a bargain?"

Snow knew better, but hoping she might spare the people of the mountain, he nodded. He looked at the apple. His favorite food. And wondered. Would he die quickly or slowly? Easily or in agony?

He didn't care. To save his new friends, his lover and his family, he would do it.

"Go ahead," she said. Her lips formed a thin smile.

Snow brought the apple to his mouth and took a bite. He held the apple bit in his mouth, not chewing.

"It would please my heart to see you eat it all," she said.

It did not taste of poison. In fact, it was sweet, juicy. He crunched down on it.

"There," she said. "You see? I've given you food. We've made a bargain. Now finish."

She watched with lifeless eyes as he took more bites, chewed and swallowed.

Nothing happened until he reached the core. The brown seeds showed through tin films of white core. He held it in his hand, looking down at it, at his fate. And that was when he felt the first onset of dizziness.

Snow looked up at her.

The old lady's smile widened. She shrugged and said, "I will not have it said by anyone, strangers, people in the village, or your friends you refuse to tell me about that I had you killed. You will be found dead of natural causes. This road is well-traveled. It will not take long before you are located."

Snow tried to take a deep breath. Failed. His lungs simply weren't working properly.

The old lady reached over him and opened the door. They had traveled only a short way. The carriage came to a stop.

She grabbed him by the upper arms with surprising strength, and yanked him forward.

He realized he had little strength in his legs. He fell to his knees. Her jeweled slipper came up. With her foot against the middle of his back, she shoved and kicked him out.

He fell onto the side of the dirt road. Rocks scraped against his shoulder and hip and the palm of his hand. He flailed, but the world began to spin and he did not recognize down from up.

In a blur, he heard the carriage clatter off. Hoof beats passed and he looked up at large horses carrying her personal guards. One by one the men passed him, each one looking down at him with no emotion.

Immediately, he heard Doc's voice in his head. The man and his knowledge had rubbed off on him. Doc often told stories from his past around the hearth. Stories about when he treated the sick, the injured. Right now, he knew Doc would tell him to throw it all up. All of it to get the poison out.

Snow had little strength left, but he managed to raise his hand to his mouth and jam his fingers inside. He had no time for hesitation. He choked himself, then coughed.

Bits of apple flew from his mouth and onto the roadside. It wasn't enough.

He did it over and over again until he flopped back in the dirt in pure exhaustion.

He had no idea if it was a good or bad sign that he was still alive. But he counted it as good. As long as there was breath inside him, there was hope.

He looked up at the sky where the clouds had turned dark gray. Sinister. He shivered.

He had the thought that if he survived the poison, he might not survive the weather.

Assessing his body, he found he could sit up again. That was a good sign. Maybe the poison had been expelled. Or enough of it, at least, that he could move again. Though weak, if he could walk he could follow the road. He could look for the brook. He could find his way home to Sleepy. To all the men.

He pushed himself up to stand. Off-balance, dizzy, it was a miracle he managed.

Slowly, he shambled down the road, catching himself from falling with each step, but forging ahead.

It seemed to take forever to go only a few steps. Determined, he kept going.

The temperature dropped.

The wind cried out in a crowd of voices, like all the world's ancient ghosts screaming at once. The early spring flowers in the gullies he passed bent and wilted under the cold press of air. A crystal of ice flicked his left cheek and his knit cap flew off his head and blew up into the wicked, black branches of a tree.

Still, Snow trudged on. His head whirled. He could not feel his limbs, yet still he stood. Still, he walked.

Two times he doubled over in dry heaves. The poison erupting within.

Bent and fighting his way through the increasing winds, he pushed upward, toward the hills. He could hear the brook now, off in the distance. And maybe even voices.

Maybe.

His stomach cramped. He winced but kept on. His strength lessened. He could hear his feet drag over every rock and rut. His knees bent. He had no more energy left. He wasn't going to make it.

He fell hard onto his knees, rolling to his back. This was bad. Very, very bad.

The wind washed over him, playing in his hair. He looked up. Eyes open. To a dark, dark sky.

It started to rain. Every drop hit his face with cold little stings, but he could not move. He could feel the rocks where he lay, poking his shoulders, back and buttocks, but he was unable to feel beyond the skin. It was as if he were hollow with no muscles and bone, nothing to move the skin that encased him.

His eyes filled with rain but he still saw waving tree branches overhead, the slant of water falling from the darkened sky, and clouds puffing up like deep bruises.

Was he even alive? He could not feel his heart or his own breathing. But the insides of his nose and throat were cool so there had to be air passing through him.

His skin grew colder.

He wanted to blink the rainwater from his eyes, but even his eyelids would not move.

If the poison didn't kill him, shock and exposure would. Ironic that he'd been rescued from murder and healed from hypothermia, only to face those two problems again so soon, and this time he would succumb.

He thought again of Sleepy and wanted to weep. The kind big man had been through so much. Sleepy deserved better.

Snow had been such a stupid boy. Going out when he'd been told over and over not to leave the house if he was alone.

He would leave behind a lot of broken hearts. He should have died in the snow at the hands of the huntsman when no one knew of him and he had no friends to miss him. He should have been bones for the wolves long before now.

A fool's death for a fool.

It was cruel that he had this time while dying to think about his whole life and everything that had happened to him in the past few weeks. Even though he had no physical pain, his thoughts were painful. He grieved for Sleepy. And for them all.

Far too slowly, the world began to fade.

Chapter Nineteen

The darkness echoed with far away voices.

"—careful, don't trip—"

"—but he can't be dead, he can't, he can't—"

"—there's breath—"

Snow's head bobbed and he realized he was being carried by someone.

"—careful, more rocks. Come this way—"

"—why, why did he, why—"

All he could see was darkness and a circle of light. Probably from a lantern carried in a hand by a person walking ahead of the person who held him.

Rain still dotted his face.

Someone sobbed once. The person carrying him leaned his head down and touched Snow's forehead with his damp cheek. Snow saw Sleepy's beautiful face marred by such anguish it hurt to look at him. And he realized it was no longer raining. What dripped against his face were tears.

He heard Doc's voice. "Up ahead. Only a little more."

"Doc, tell me again he isn't dead!" Sleepy clutched Snow tightly to his chest.

Snow wanted to speak, but none of his muscles, including voice, throat and mouth worked.

"He isn't dead."

"But can you make him well again?"

"Hush. Wait until we get home. It's not far now. And I'll examine him and try to assess what happened. It could be anything."

Poison! Snow wanted to yell. But he could not utter even the smallest sound.

He felt cold through and through. Sleepy's warm arms and chest barely seemed to touch him.

More voices came through the darkness, and more round spaces of light appeared in the air like bobbing, glowing flowers. Snow's head was tilted away from Sleepy's chest, so he could see dim shapes ahead, and men moving. Men running.

"Hey. Over here. He's been found!"

"Thank the fates!"

"Is he alive?"

"Yes! So far."

Doc's voice. "Run ahead and get the water on to heat."

Though Snow could feel nothing, their familiar voices brought him mental comfort.

At least now he would not die alone. Unknown. A mystery never solved. They'd found him. And they would care for his body, make sure it had a decent grave.

Snow saw through blurred vision the yard in front of their home, the hill, the tree on the hill and the round wooden door.

They'd arrived.

He had a brief thought of the cat. What had happened to Sil?

Then he forgot about her as the bustle of getting him through the little door and down into the front room became somewhat of a drama. The last time they had him slung over one man's shoulder, but this time Sleepy held him against his chest.

Sleepy turned sideways to get them down the little hall where the walls sprouted thin pale roots from the plants on the mound.

Everything smelled of earth and fire, and scared and sweaty young men.

Soon they were home. Snow saw the hearth burning merrily and a pot over the flames to boil water.

He saw the long wooden table shining from where he had polished and cleaned it before he and Sil had taken their forsaken journey.

And there, sitting on that table, watching with wide green eyes, sat Sil safe and sound.

Snow was grateful. For she was a beloved pet and he hated to think she was lost out there in the rainy, summer wood.

Sleepy rushed Snow to their bed.

"Careful, careful." Doc came around and put his hand under Snow's neck and head. Together they set him on the tops of the covers.

Gentle hands began to undress him.

Doc's hands moved to his head, fingers probing, probably feeling for wounds.

"He hasn't hit his head that I can see," Doc said.

Sleepy had Snow's shirt unbuttoned. Together they lifted his shoulders and got it off. Snow could see the other men gather around. Curious. Worried. They shifted foot to foot, their boots creaking. It was the oddest sound.

Snow tried to blink and couldn't. His eyes felt very dry.

Doc examined Snow's chest and rolled him to look at his back. "No wounds," he announced.

They moved lower. Sleepy undid Snow's trouser buttons and parted the fabric. Together, he and Doc lifted Snow's hips and slid the material down. Sleepy moved further down the bed and undid his bootstraps, pulling the boots off one by one.

Soon, Snow lay naked before all the men, pale and unmoving. Like the dead.

Doc's fingers were gentle as he examined every part of him. "He's not snake-bit. I see no rashes or injuries. There is no fever. He's alive but he simply cannot move."

Snow saw the shadowy forms of the men move about him in confusion. His senses all still worked. He heard their breaths, their distressed voices. He smelled the day's dust upon them, the tartness of hard work, and the aired blankets upon which he lay, freshly laundered by him the previous day.

He felt the softness of those blankets against his back, and the respectful probing of Doc's fingers as he searched again for a reason for Snow's death-like stillness.

Doc actually apologized before he put his fingers against Snow's lips and probed his mouth. "His airway is clear."

"I'm sorry," Doc said again as he turned him and probed other areas he'd missed in the first examination, including between the cheeks of his buttocks.

Doc straightened up, his glasses like round gold disks shimmering upon his face. "He appears to be in perfect health."

Sleepy let out a sad, anguished sound. "He's not moving!"

Snow watched Doc touch Sleepy on the forearm. "We will care for him. Maybe it will pass."

Sleepy pulled a folded blanket up over Snow's frozen form. He took his hand in his own strong palm, and sat on the side of the bed looking down at him.

Doc stood beside him. "We should close his eyes so they don't dry out."

Sleepy reached up and put his fingertip against one of Snow's eyelids, pushing it down. It slid over his eye, then bounced back up.

Doc tried, very gently, to close the other eye, and the same thing happened. Snow's eyes wouldn't close.

"We will keep a damp rag over his eyes at night. It will help. But if he's awake in there, inside his body, we should assume that he can also see. And cutting off that sense from him would be cruel."

"Do you think he's awake?"

Doc shrugged. "He could be. He might hear us, too. In which case we need to talk to him every day, let him know we're here for him. It could pass by morning. I cannot say what has happened to him for sure, but there's something about this that reminds me of another patient. I can't recall—"

"Try, Doc." Sleepy's face was broken. "Please. Try to remember. What was it?"

Doc shook his head. "I'll think on it."

With all his might, Snow tried to project to them an image of the old lady, the queen. The apple. How he ate it and fell.

But there was no magic that would help him communicate to them. At least not for him. He needed to get his voice back and that might never happen. And then they would never know what truly happened.

If only he had not left the cave. Then Sil would not have gotten out. And he would not have chased her.

He ran the scenario in his head over and over again. The cat. Becoming lost. But he hadn't been away for more than ten minutes. He had not wandered too far, for the men had found him quite quickly, it seemed, even in the storm.

And that was when he decided he had probably been carefully watched, off and on, since the moment Doc and his men had rescued him from the huntsman.

The old lady knew he had lived!

And the queen was a patient woman who always got what she wanted in the end. This was her plan. To find him and poison him. She had lain in wait for him to be confident enough to go out on his own. Her men watched. Waited. And today had been the perfect day. She'd been out on her rounds delivering food and poisoned apples to the poor. She'd been culling her trash.

Snow had fallen right into her murderous white-gloved hands.

He should have known she would never let him go until she was sure he was dead. She couldn't do it in her palace and leave any trace for the servants to find. She needed to have him taken away. Killed and left for the wolves. But when that had failed, her plan needed a rewrite. She knew he could not survive alone. That meant he'd been seen and helped by people in her land, strangers, but still harmful if they talked. If they spread rumors he was alive.

Her poison for the poor was the perfect solution. It left illness and death. The bodies gave no indication of foul play. Their deaths were always ruled as a natural cause. People died every day. Their hearts stopped. Their brains stopped. If the prince was found dead by no foul play, she would have her vindication, and her power would remain unthreatened.

Why she'd kept Snow alive for two years confounded him. She'd wanted a royal child. That could have been her main reason. But Snow had also liked to think she could not bring herself to murder him outright. That there might be some heart in her amidst her greed. But now he knew he'd been naïve. A fool. She'd never had a heart. She excelled at manipulation, punishment and reward for herself. Nothing more.

Tears welled in his eyes.

Sleepy jerked. "Look! He's crying. He can hear us. He is awake!"

Doc came and looked down at him. "Bring water," he ordered over his shoulder.

"Snow, Snow, can you hear me?" Sleepy crooned in his ear. "We're all here. We'll all help you. You can survive this. You can! I know it!" Then he leaned in and kissed him softly on the lips.

Snow felt more tears swell within him. But he still could not move.

The other men came around the bed and touched the blankets. Their murmured encouragement lifted his thoughts from the depths they threatened to slip into. He was loved. He was wanted. And they would do all they could to make him live.

Exhausted, he fell into deep sleep.

*

He was eating apples. A whole basketful. Red and glossy and round. There were too many, but someone told him he had to keep eating. And eating. Until the basket was empty. He began to vomit.

Snow woke lying on his back. Staring upward.

Sleepy lay curled against him, warm and comforting. The bigger man was fully dressed on top of the blanket. His breath came slow and even.

Snow heard voices. The word *catatonic.* He tried to move but couldn't.

He saw men out the corner of his eye. Hap, Sneezy, Dope. Sitting at the table. Doc sat at the head of the table. He had something in his hand. A book. He was reading one of his thick medical books which he kept by the side of his bed. Snow knew this. He'd even paged through one once while cleaning, amazed at all the information it contained.

"—an immobile or unresponsive stupor. There is a muscular rigidity, a daze to the eyes, yet the person can be conscious. Causes: Fever. Mental aberration. Neurological injury. Poison."

Yes! That's me! Snow wanted to scream it out to them.

Doc read a little more which Snow did not follow, then sat back and closed the book.

"What does it mean, Doc?" Dope asked.

"He has no fever. He is not mentally ill. I can find no head injury."

"Then all that leaves is poison. Could he have eaten something?" Sneezy asked.

"Maybe. Or maybe something broke inside his brain that no one can understand."

"He was healthy when we left him to go to work," Hap said.

"Yes."

"He was lying on the side of the road when we found him." Hap leaned forward. "Like someone just dropped him there. Maybe someone broke in and took him."

"There is no sign of forced entry. He opened that door," Doc said.

Dope continued the speculation. "And someone was there. They took him. Poisoned him. Then dropped him in the road to die."

Doc scratched at the back of his head the way he did while deep in thought.

Beside Snow, Sleepy's breathing changed. Snow knew he was awake.

Sleepy lifted his tousled head and put his hand in the center of Snow's chest.

"Snow," he whispered softly. "I'm here. Are you awake?"

Yes. And I love you so much. I'm so sorry I opened the door and went out. So sorry.

"I know you didn't mean to get yourself into trouble. But I wish you could tell me what happened to you."

The old lady! It was the queen!

"If you can hear me, I'm not going to leave your side."

But you have to work!

"I will stay home from work for as long as it takes to get you well."

You can't. I'm dying.

"You're not dying. I know in my heart you are awake and aware. All we need to do is get your body going again. We'll figure this out."

Sleepy's eyes were a light, soft brown this morning. His morning beard made his face look chiseled and sharp, but nothing about him was sharp or hurtful. Sleepy was the kindest, most gentle man Snow had ever met.

I love you.

"I love you," Sleepy whispered, and kissed him again.

Snow screamed inside, wanting out of this prison of his body, wanting to put his arms around Sleepy and hold him tight.

His anguish was interrupted when he heard a chair tip over.

Doc was standing in the middle of the room between the table and the bed, his hands rubbing together. "I remember something now."

Sleepy sat up. "Doc?"

"These symptoms. Years ago I encountered them in a child I'd gone to the aid of. You remember, Bash?"

Bash had just come in from the back. He stood silhouetted in the firelight.

"What?"

"Years ago. Before we met Hap and the rest of you. We were walking through a village. There was a six year old girl—"

Snow listened intently.

146

"I remember," Bash said. "Her mother was crying, asking anyone about for help. We went into her house but Doc, I also remember there was nothing you could do for the child."

"There was no detectable reason why that child should have died. But she had the same symptoms. Catatonia. A healthy six year old does not fall into a stupor without a reason. I remember asking her mother if she knew what might have happened. The girl had no injuries, no illness. She was healthy that morning. All the mother said was that the queen had been in town giving food to the poor."

"The queen—" Bash slammed his hand down on the table. "That's—you're right."

"Remember the rumors? No one could prove it," Doc said.

"What rumors?" Dope asked.

Bash turned to him with an angry face. "That the queen poisons a small percentage of the food to slowly cull the poor from the face of the earth."

Yes, you're on the right track. Snow was yelling in his head.

"Do you remember any more from that day, Bash?" Doc asked.

"Yeh." Bash walked over to the bed where Snow and Sleepy lay. He looked down at Snow. He put his hand on his shoulder. "The girl's mother said she hadn't eaten her breakfast. So when the queen arrived, she was hungry. The first thing the girl ate was an apple. It was spring, and apples were out of season, so it was a fine treat."

"Apples!" Sleepy sat up. "Snow loves apples."

That's it. You all are geniuses. You figured it out! Snow wanted to laugh and cry. To hug them all and kiss Sleepy until he couldn't breathe.

Doc came to the bed and Bash stepped back. He put his hand on Snow's forehead and looked deeply into his eyes, his spectacles glowing. "Snow, did you see the queen? Is that what happened? Did you eat something? An apple, maybe?"

Snow's eyes welled. *Yes. Oh, yes!* Tears slid down the sides of his eyes, hot, then cooling at his temples.

Doc looked at Sleepy over Snow's still gaze. "I'll take that as a yes."

Thank you, Doc. Thank you, Bash. All of you!

"He's been poisoned. Now we know it! Doc, can you help him?"

Bash turned away.

Doc stepped back, sighing. "I'll do everything I can."

By the tone of Doc's voice, Snow knew he was still at a loss. The mystery of the poison was still not solved. It could be any number of poisons. And not all poisons had antidotes.

Chapter Twenty

Something weighted but small pressed against Snow's right leg. He tried to see but could not. But when he heard the purr, there was no doubt.

Sil was curled up with him in his bed.

Someone was sitting up beside him, a cup in their hand, staring off at the shadows on the rock walls. Sleepy. At Snow's side like he'd always been there. And always would be.

Something was going on in the front room. Raised voices.

Sleepy was ignoring them. But suddenly, as if sensing Snow had been asleep and was now awake, Sleepy turned to him and began to softly speak.

"If you come back to me, Snow, I'll treat you like the rarest jewel. I will defend you until I can't walk and I can't see. Until I am dust. I promise I will be true. I will name every flower I see after you. I will call the moon your soul and never forget you. Not for one minute of any day. I'll give you everything I earn, everything I have. All my thoughts, my words, my dreams. I will give you my heart to do with as you please. Anything and everything. But you must come back to me. Please, please, come back."

I will try to come back. I will try. Sleepy, I love you.

In the front room, more raised voices, but Snow concentrated on Sleepy.

"I will tell you every funny story I can think of. I will tell you every day how beautiful you are. I will make love to you in beds, on couches, in gardens and under the moon. I will brush your hair. I will give you the food from my plate."

I want to give you all of that, too!

Metal clanked against metal.

Hap's voice. "Wait, you fool. He's saying goodbye."

"I will savor you. I will memorize you. I will hold you. I will live only in the language of your heart. I will love you, Snow, until the very stars themselves die."

Snow wanted to cry again, but his eyes were so dry.

"But now." Sleepy's voice lowered and there was a sob caught on the currents of the tone. "Now, I must fight for you. I will fight for you."

He got up and Snow watched him walked around to the end of the bed, heard him rummage through his chest of clothes. Heard the rattle of the swords and knives.

No. Sleepy.

Sleepy stood, buckling on harness after harness. Two swords and an uncounted number of knives were buckled on, shoved into his boots, his waistband, his gauntlet. He wore a leather vest, and gauntlets carved with swirls of leaves.

Snow knew what was happening. Out the corner of his eye, he saw the glint of metal, so much metal, in the front room. Heard the clanging as the men walked, as they prepared.

They were going to fight. For him.

No, Sleepy. No! You said you would never leave my side! You said—

Snow's thoughts choked in new grief. He would lose them. He would lose them all, for no one could stand against the queen and her guard.

"The plan has been made," Hap said. "Dusk we meet at the edge of the wood beyond Hans' farm."

With all his might, Snow called to Sleepy. *Come back. Come back!*

But Sleepy, in all the glory of his leathers and gear, his weapons and his determination, turned away.

Then he walked with the others, single file, up the narrow passage. Snow heard the little door open. Heard the men step out, the rustling of their battle cloaks, their leathers creaking, their weapons jingling.

Everyone left but Doc, who stayed behind to care for Snow.

If they fought for him and died, and if he lived, he would not be able to bear it.

He cried out in his mind until he had no more thoughts, until there was nothing. No sound. No vision. No hope left.

*

When Snow climbed up to consciousness again, Doc was sitting by his side. The shadows flickered on the walls. Doc's specs glittered.

"Are you awake?" Doc asked. "You're eyes are filling up."

Snow was grateful Doc was paying attention.

Doc took a wet cloth and wiped Snow's tears, then soaked Snow's lips and wrung the cloth a little. He sprinkled a few drops of water into Snow's dry mouth. Water. His body wanted more. But it had to be slow this way, for he could not swallow.

"I tried to purge you, but there was nothing left inside you. Do you remember?"

Snow did not.

"You did it yourself, didn't you?"

Snow sent the thought of a nod in his direction.

The silence in the little home was too silent.

The men were gone. It came back to him quickly why they'd gone. And how most likely it was to their deaths.

All because of him. For him. He had been born a cursed prince. As a cursed prince he would die. And so would they all.

He shuddered.

Doc looked down at him. "Snow?"

What? Of course he could not answer.

"Did you just move?"

I don't think so.

"I think your body gave a little shiver," Doc said. "I have done nothing for you but maybe your body is getting well on its own. If it can shed the rest of the poison—" He paused and scratched the back of his head. "If only I could get more water into you. Wash it from your system."

But what did Snow have to live for?

Sleepy and the others had gone off to get themselves killed.

Doc brought another cool cloth and washed Snow's face. "There, do you feel that? Can you try to move for me?

Snow was still naked under the blanket. Cold. He could feel nothing but the surface of his skin where the blanket touched him, and where the bed met his back.

Doc pushed back the blanket until the side of Snow's chest was revealed. He picked up his limp arm, meeting his palm with his own hand.

"Try to move a finger. Anything. Concentrate. Focus."

I'm trying. In his mind, Snow's eyebrows narrowed, his lips pressed tight, his neck muscles tensed. He directed his will to his fingers. Thought: *Flex.*

Doc squeezed his hand. Snow could feel that but nothing more. "Again. Try."

Snow concentrated with all his energy.

"Yes! Your little finger twitched! I knew you were in there. I knew you could hear me." Doc leaned over into Snow's face. "And see me." Through the lenses of Doc's glasses the intense eyes brimmed.

A twitch. It wasn't enough. Snow needed to get up. To find the men. All of them. Everyone who was gathering, banding together. He needed to order them to stop, or fight alongside them. Either way, this was not good enough. He felt useless lying in bed unable to move. And what if he only recovered some movement and not all? It terrified him almost as much as dying.

Doc said, "I can tell by the color in your cheeks you are anxious. Worried. You must try to be calm. The more you struggle, the more your body can fight against you."

Snow blinked.

Doc's smile turned to a wide grin. "Do you know what you just did? You blinked!"

Snow had not even tried. It just happened. A warmth suffused his body in utter relief. Slowly, his terror faded. But he still worried.

Sleepy was out there. Along with Hap, Bash, Sneezy, Dope and Grump. And countless others risking their lives because they hated the queen. Now they had someone else to back. Snow.

He reevaluated his position. He definitely had a reason to live. To hope. But at what cost?

As the evening wore on, Doc never left Snow's side. He wiped down his face with warm water. Then his whole body.

Snow let Doc's ministrations soak in and fill him up with tenderness. Doc rubbed oil on his feet and Snow concentrated on the essence of it soaking into him. It left his skin tingling not in a painful way, but a good way.

Doc moved his hands up and down Snow's legs. He massaged his hips, then each arm, and his shoulders. Over and over again he ran his hands over Snow's motionless body. First with warm water and cloth, then with oil and his hands. It warmed him. From deep inside, a place inside Snow began to stir, to spark. A flame low and tight in his solar plexus.

Snow tried to think only of Doc's hands, the warmth, the affection and the trust. But he could not stop wondering about where Sleepy and the others had gone into the night with all their weapons. And what they might be doing.

Many times his eyes overflowed with tears.

With soft reassuring murmurs, Doc wiped them away.

It seemed hours had passed. Snow could now move his right foot and hand. He could blink. He could swallow but not speak. But that meant Doc could now give him water, and he drank half a cup with Doc supporting his head.

If Doc had been right and he needed to wash the poison from his system, the water might make things go faster. He hoped.

It was agonizingly slow work, as if Doc were carving Snow's body out of rock or ice and into living essence a little at a time.

Several times, Doc turned Snow's body so he could work on his back and the backs of his legs and arms. He massaged Snow's scalp and neck.

Surely the man's hands must be cramped by now, Snow thought. But Doc never faltered.

He broke only rarely to drink water and eat some bread.

When the fire burned low, Doc took a quick break to build it up.

"Dawn is coming," Doc said when he returned from the hearth.

Snow made a small noise, like a moan.

Doc touched his forehead. "I know it seems slow, but you are recovering quite nicely."

Another hour passed, the candle on the bed stand burning low, and Snow was ready to sit up a little with pillows propped against his back. Doc helped him. Snow bent a knee all by himself and the adrenalin rush through his muscles and veins gave him tingling feelings all over, inside and out, until he was trembling.

Snow's first words were, "Sleepy."

"I know," Doc said, mouth down-turned. "You're worried."

Snow's head bowed in a single nod. All he could manage.

"It may seem like an impulsive thing, this action, the men leaving with their swords and knives, going into the night. But this has been in the planning stages for a long, long time. You are the catalyst, yes. Their outrage over the second attempted murder of you fueled their blood, but their rage and their anger and their grief for—for everything that has happened to them and to you is not some wild urge. This has been coming for years. Liaisons. Connections. Plans."

Doc's steady voice gave Snow something to center on. He could see within his mind all the stories the men had told that night weeks ago around the hearth fire, how driven they all were by personal pain, and by what Doc was always saying about the right way to live.

Those stories replayed, moving visions upon the landscape of his thoughts. Horror stories all. Sick families. Death. Murder. Sleepy's sister being kidnapped, his parents murdered before his eyes.

They all had reasons to fight. It wasn't all and only about Snow.

Snow opened his mouth. "I will fight, too." Only the words came out more like, "Ah ill ight, oo."

Doc understood him.

"You worry so. I don't blame you." Doc stroked his limbs again with warm water.

Snow could make a weak fist with his left hand.

"I am afraid they will all die," Snow said with a bit more articulation this time.

"Tonight is for meetings. Lots of meetings. Sending messages. Setting traps. No one will be fighting yet, I hope. But the men are prepared if that should befall them. And when they all return for a hot meal and a bed, they will be so happy to see you up and talking."

Snow tried to offer up a smile, but feared a grimace was all he could muster.

"So now that you can talk, what did happen to you today?"

Snow shut his eyes in shame. "I needed water."

He proceeded to tell Doc about the cat escaping and how he gave chase.

"The carriage came up fast. The guards seemed to appear from nothing right out of the woods. I'm sorry. I'm sorry I was such a fool to even start to go out that door."

"No. Don't be." Doc hushed him. "It is wrong to keep one such as you locked away."

"But you didn't. I went out on weekends and at dusk."

Doc shook his head. "To leave you all alone five days a week… of course you would be tempted to feel safe enough to do a simple thing like get some water. I should have known. We all should have taken much better care of you."

Snow shook his head. "Never say that. You have all taken the best care of me!"

"You're our prince. We should have watched over you every hour of every day. Each taking turns to stay home with you."

"But even then," Snow said. "The queen would have found a way. She always gets her way."

"Yes, she does at that," Doc said as if he knew more than he was saying.

The candle sizzled and went out. Doc lit another from the hearth and brought it over to the bed.

"The queen told me she's been waiting all this time. She knew I was in this area."

"She has a lot of spies. Which is why we were careful to disguise you."

Snow nodded. "I remembered your stories around the hearth. I threw it all up. The apple. But her poison worked fast."

"You are very smart to do that." Doc patted his shoulder. "Do you think you can eat something now?" he asked.

"I'll try." Snow wanted to get stronger fast.

Doc boiled him some broth and brought him warm bread and butter.

Snow ate most of it, his mouth so dry he could barely swallow. But he managed.

Just as Doc was setting aside Snow's plate for him, a sound came from above the hill, and they heard the door thump open.

Jangling. Low voices. Boot steps.

Doc smiled at Snow. "See? They're back safe and sound."

The first to come through the passage was Hap.

"I'm so hungry I could eat a bear!" he exclaimed.

Next came Grump. "What? No dinner set out?"

Bash and Sneezy and Dope followed.

Where was Sleepy?

Snow made a strangled, anguished sound.

They all turned to look at him.

"He's up!" Hap exclaimed. "Sleepy, get your ass down here!"

Sleepy practically ran into the room and straight into Snow's arms.

"Thank you, Doc. Thank you!" Sleepy took Snow into his arms, nearly lifting him off the bed. His sheathed swords poked Snow, and all the belts he wore, and the hard gauntlets.

But Snow laughed, luxuriating in the feel of his lover's arms around him. He had so much to say to him. So much to share. To reassure.

Into Sleepy's ear, Snow whispered, "I heard everything you said to me."

Sleepy made a low sound, then kissed him on the neck as he held him tightly to his chest.

Over Sleepy's shoulder, Snow saw all the others lined up, gazing at them with pure affection on their faces. Even Grump's usual frown had lifted to a smile.

They all took turns patting Doc on the back. But Doc would not take credit for Snow's rehabilitation.

"It's our prince who is the brave one. And smart. When he knew he was poisoned, he forced up what he'd eaten. It saved him."

"You saved me when you found me. Otherwise, I would be bones in the nests of wolves," Snow said.

Soon the evening routine began. The men sharing the chores, the cooking, the setting of the table, the putting away of weapons and cloaks in their right places.

Doc said, "So tell me what happened. Is there another plan for tonight?"

Sleepy and Snow were left to themselves for a few minutes.

Snow said, "I was so worried when you all ran out with your swords. I thought you'd die."

Sleepy rubbed his jaw against the top of Snow's head. "We are preparing to fight. And we'll continue to fight. Until you are on the throne."

"But I pictured—you know—actual combat."

"Soon. It will happen. But we are smart and we have lots of contacts, double agents, spies, people who have turned who are close to the queen. We are so ready. We've been preparing for years."

"Years? But I was only eighteen two years ago when I was imprisoned."

"Yes, but we were already suffering. The land, the villages, the poor. We formed an underground long before you were of age for the throne. Mostly it was to help defend the farmers and others from the queen's guard. So what happened to me wouldn't happen to anyone else. But when your death was announced, we planned for a future rebellion. There were rumors you weren't really dead, and our underground grew."

"For me?"

Sleepy nodded. "Somewhat. We suspected you were alive. We had intelligence within the palace and that confirmed it. They had seen you. But even if the queen had succeeded in killing you, we still had our plan. She would be taken down. She had to go. Luckily, you weren't dead, and we ambushed your attacker."

Snow explained, as he had to Doc, how he had been taken prisoner a second time. And how he had been poisoned.

"I'm sorry I wasn't there for you," Sleepy said.

"Doc apologized, too. But none of you should. You have been my best friends and cared for me more than anyone has my entire life since my mother died. Please. If I can give one order to you, stop apologizing."

Sleepy cupped Snow's face in his both palms and kissed him on the lips.

Snow's mouth opened to him. So much had happened in such a short time. How he'd missed him! His pine scent, the fresh tang of him, night still sticking to him like rain, like wind.

Sleepy's hands ran down his back and it was only then Snow remembered he was naked, sitting there before all the men for all to see. But that was how they were living in such close confines. Open and unashamed. Fearless with their affections. Brazen with their bodies and their love.

Snow felt right at home.

When their morning *supper* was ready, Sleepy helped Snow into his red cloak and steered him to the table.

"Are you hungry?" asked Doc, who still worriedly checked on him every five minutes.

"Yes," Snow said. And he was. The poison was gone now. He felt a normal appetite.

Chapter Twenty-One

After the meal, the men slept the day away.

Snow asked Sleepy, who held him tightly in his arms, "Will their jobs wait?"

"Yes. Most of the others who work the quarry are like us. Including our supervisor. They understand we were out all night and need to sleep for what is to come?"

"And what is to come?" Snow asked.

"There will be a disarming of the queen's guard. Tonight we approach the palace."

Snow's skin shivered at the thought. He knew he would return some day, if he survived. Just not so soon.

"And fighting?"

"We hope it will be peaceful and quick. But yes, I expect there will be some struggles and frays."

Snow hoped not. Too much blood had been spilled because of Serena. And his seven men? He could not stand the thought of any of them being hurt or killed.

He could tell Sleepy was exhausted, embracing his nickname to the fullest, but Snow felt like they'd been apart for an eternity. So much had happened and he had not been able to talk, to tell Sleepy about his thoughts.

"Everything you said to me while I was paralyzed was—is so, um—" He fought for the words. "Shattering."

"Oh, that's—"

"No, shh! I mean in a good way. Sleepy, you break my heart I love you so much. And all those things you said, I can't even believe how lucky I am. I wanted to respond but I couldn't. Now I can."

"You don't need to respond. You already do in every smile you give me, every kiss."

Snow smiled. "Through fate and pain and suffering I found you. The best of the best. And I would go through it all again to keep you."

Sleepy nuzzled his lips across Snow's in a precious, loving gesture that took Snow's breath. The kiss was not only about arousal, but communicated like a brush from beyond a soul-felt commitment.

Snow said into the kiss, "I've come back to you and I answer yes to everything. Everything you said. I would have you at my side forever."

"And I will be there. Always."

Their arms tightened about one another. Exhausted from all that had happened, they fell quickly to sleep, breath to breath, heart to heart.

*

Clattering pots and pans. The smell of sizzling potatoes. And new-baked bread.

The shadows dancing on the walls were golden this evening.

Snow had awakened groggy, but after one cup of coffee, a quickly shared sponge bath with Sleepy, and a cursory check-over from Doc, he was feeling quite normal after his major ordeal the previous day.

The men ate heartily, but quickly. They were already preparing to go out again. Into the night. Putting into place their final plans.

The Palace would be over-run by dawn.

Snow did not ask if the rebels meant to imprison the queen, or kill her. He had no qualms about her death, for she had tried twice to kill him in quite cruel ways. But thinking about it made him edgy.

As they dressed in their leathers and fastened their sword-belts, Snow dressed, too. Yesterday's clothes were filthy and torn, but he had another set given to him only a week ago by all the men. They were not loaned. These were new. Brought home with supplies from one of the nearby villages.

Snow looked at Sleepy, who was examining which knives he wanted to take.

"I was taught the sword for five years, as every prince should be taught. The queen put a stop to it when I was fifteen, unbeknownst to my father. But I still remember how—"

Sleepy looked up. "You're not going with us, though."

Snow frowned. "I am going."

"No."

Doc and Bash came over to Sleepy's alcove, their gauntlets only half laced.

"What's the problem?" Doc faced Sleepy when he asked the question.

"There is no problem," Snow said, stepping forward. "I'm going with you all."

"He'll be safer if he stays here," Sleepy said to Doc, ignoring Snow's statement.

Doc turned to Snow. "You don't agree."

Snow shook his head. "I can handle a sword. I've simply never gotten the chance."

"You're not considering this, Doc." Sleepy squared his shoulders.

Doc ignored the challenging stance. "I think it should be Snow's decision."

"You can't possibly mean that!"

"I'm going. I can help," Snow insisted. "Plus, you can prove to all we meet that I am real. I am alive."

Dope sauntered over to the group. "I think that sounds fair."

Sleepy took a fast step toward Dope, shoulders back, chest out, his arms coming up. "No one asked your opinion!"

Doc put up his hand between them, palm facing Sleepy's chest, almost touching but stopping just an inch short. "Cease!"

Dope took several steps back.

The others turned from the front room and stared.

Snow reached out and put his hand on Sleepy's forearm, gripping tight. Trying to get him to look at him.

"Sleepy, I need to do this!" Snow said.

Sleepy backed off, took a step back. His face was a storm of anger. His eyes, no longer soft and caring, were almost black with an inner rage. "I just got you back! I'm not losing you again!"

The change had been so abrupt. One minute Sleepy was calm, adoring, happy. The next his past seemed to seep from his pores. Anguish ruled him. Fury. He wanted to fight. He needed to fight.

Snow was not a part of that world his lover had now entered, except for Sleepy's need to keep him safe. Sleepy had not been able to keep his sister, Keri, safe. And he had almost lost Snow less than one day ago. Snow realized all of this as he read Sleepy's body language, watched him fume, listened to his tone.

"Sleepy, look at me." Snow stroked down his arm until he could clasp his hand with his own. Sleepy's fingers remained limp.

Sleepy shook his head at him. "I won't risk you. I won't!"

"I know what you're saying," Snow said softly. "I understand where it's coming from."

Brows furrowed, the corners of his mouth down-turned, Sleepy said, "If you understand, then you know why you should stay behind. And it's not just about what I want. You're the prince. Your life cannot be risked!"

"Sit with me for a minute." Snow nodded toward their bed. "Let's talk."

Sleepy ripped his hand from Snow's grip. "No! There is nothing to talk about." He stalked past Doc and Bash, glared at Dope, and stood for a moment by the passage that led up to their door.

"Sleepy!" Snow called out.

The big man turned. "You'll all do what you want anyway. I'll be outside."

No one stopped him as he clomped up to the door. It opened, then shut. A wind blew in, ruffling the hearth fire.

Snow let out a small moan and started forward.

Doc blocked him. "Let him go. He'll be fine. He has old scars, as do we all, but you have made him vulnerable again."

"I didn't mean—"

Doc held up his hand again. "I am not saying that's a bad thing. He's just afraid and he doesn't know how to encompass that."

"We're all scared, of course," Sneezy said. "Sleepy's right. The prince should be protected at all costs."

Grump stepped forward. "I agree. If the prince dies in battle, what will we be fighting for?"

Snow stepped into the room's brighter glow. "Anything better than this," he said. "That's what you're fighting for. Even an empty throne is better than an evil queen."

"Snow's right," Hap said. "We're fighting a new path. Even if it's not perfectly drawn, we need to take it. We need to try."

"But why risk the prince?" Dope asked.

"You're not risking me. I told you I can fight. I can help. And my presence—will it not inspire those who aren't sure, who've never met me as you all have?"

Bash nodded. "We all—all of us gathering tonight—need something to fight for. Something we can see. And this is Snow's battle, too. Doc is right when he says it's Snow's decision, not ours. In the end, he needs to do what his heart tells him. Not us. Not Sleepy. But his own heart."

They all turned to Snow. It was amazing how energized he felt, how healthy after being so incapacitated. His blood flowed strong. His vision was clear, chin up. The men stood around him, all staring at him. All waiting.

There was power here. Reason. For the first time in Snow's life he needed to take the title with which he'd been born and own it. He wanted to make it count for something. He was a prince. He'd been forced to be invisible, then a prisoner and a plaything, and finally tossed aside like a pail full of offal.

His dreams had been diminished. Broken and scattered like snowflakes to melt in the sun.

He looked around at his new friends.

Bash and Doc, so kind, lovers who found each other in the worst of strife. Doc had been the wise man for him. The healer.

Sneezy and Grump, another couple who'd found each other, eased each other from rough time to new hope for life, family and love.

Dope who loved to be organized, who was loyal as only a true brother could be, and who made damn fine potato cakes.

And Hap who never had a bad word for anyone. He saw the light everywhere he went.

These men together represented the whole of what they were fighting for. All parts of a bigger design, the aspects of a humanity who deserved some fairness in life, some hope in all the bleakness.

And Sleepy. Sleepy, too, the man who would give the shirt off his back for a boy stranger cold and in need, empty and broken and alone. Who said he would give all his earnings, his thoughts, his dreams, his heart. That he would name every flower he saw after Snow.

Sleepy embodied everything they were fighting for. Hearth. Home. Happiness. And most of all, love.

"We need to do this," Snow said. "I need to. I need to be there with all of you to fight and show all of them, everyone who wants to fight, why we do this. Why it's necessary. You all gave everything to me, sacrificed for me, risked your lives for me. Now it's my turn. Now I need to give back. To prove it's all been worth it."

"Yes!" Hap grinned.

The others all nodded, and made sounds of agreement. They surrounded Snow. A whoop went up from Sneezy to Hap to Dope.

"You can use this?" Bash handed Snow a longsword, silver metal with a leather wrapped hilt.

"Yes. And a short sword, too."

Grump handed him one. Both were in leather sheaths attached to belts.

They helped him buckle them on.

His main belt, also borrowed, held a leathern bottle for water, an empty pouch (no doubt used for coin) and a red tassel made of yarn. Someone's good luck charm?

Snow had never worn heavy belts like these at his waist. It felt good. Like power. Like change. But also like death which could not be helped.

Snow donned his red, wool-lined cloak which had once belonged to Sleepy and was a little long for him, but well-loved.

Doc reached out and straightened the hood, the top of his hand grazing Snow's pale hair. "You look like a prince."

"Then so do we all," Snow replied.

The men laughed. The mirth was tinged with nerves. The energy flowed high.

Together they trudged in single file, with Doc leading, up the passage to the front door and out into the waiting night.

Chapter Twenty-Two

A high wind scurried through the tops of the trees. Though it was very dark, with no moon so far, the mountain rising beyond their path and the wood, still nine-tenths snow-covered, sent its white glow into the sky to dim the starlight. Their path wound brown and sure before them until it disappeared into the thicker ink of trees.

Four of the men held lanterns on sticks which made wedges of the path suddenly light up, baring sticks and rocks frozen in their own half graves upon the earth.

Snow came out of their home last and turned to shut the door.

"Careful not to let the cat out," Hap half-joked.

Snow gave him a single, "Ha."

But truly, it was not funny.

He saw a hunched form by a tree up the path and surmised from the height and the shoulders that it was Sleepy. None too happy. But he was waiting for them. Loyal as a summer sun. Laden with leather, swords and knives.

It was cold.

The rains of the evening before had left most of the snow melted, and sections of mudflats.

Everything smelled of dew and new green weeds. Lightning bugs sparkled the thick air.

Snow walked toward Sleepy, half-afraid that Sleepy would tell him to go home. Or worse, ignore him.

Instead, Sleepy turned toward him. Silent. A large protective presence. Wordlessly, they walked side by side, following the others on the path into the wood.

Their arms through their cloaks brushed. Barely.

Snow wanted to speak, to tell him all his thoughts. But dared not. The woods were dark, and they needed to move as stealthily as they could. No talking. No bumbling about.

Snow was not tired after his poisoning illness. Instead, he felt more alert than ever. Vision clear. Mind bright with ideas, words, past lessons coming back to him. The white terror of the queen. This was right, and this was the way to defeat her.

164

They walked for about a half an hour at a rather rapid pace. Then suddenly Doc held up his hand enough for the others to see. They all stopped.

An owl kept asking, "Who?"

All around them, the woods began to move. Figures in cloaks emerged as if from the trees themselves.

Wings swept the air—the owl annoyed, or frightened away.

Doc spoke low. "Good evening and high hails."

Quiet murmurs answered.

There had to be a hundred men or more. Maybe some were women, too. Swords gleamed in the lantern-light. Flashes of eyes. Of rivets on leather. Of buckles and cloak clasps.

Unlike Snow, most of the figures wore short cloaks, the better for battle.

But Snow had had no choice. He would cast his cloak off, if need be, though he hated to lose it, his gift from Sleepy.

Snow heard a low voice ask, "Did the prince survive?"

"The prince is healthy and with us," Doc replied.

Snow stepped forward and threw back the hood of his cloak to show his namesake, pale hair. Beneath the wool, he was shaking with his own reveal, the newness of it all. The idea that as a prince, he must act like one.

"I survived the queen's second assassination attempt. But I could not have done it without these men. And I am grateful to you all for showing up tonight."

Sleepy stepped closer to him. Always protective, even if still seething. Still hurting.

Something Snow did not expect began to happen. All around in the moonless wood, the dozens of figures that had silently appeared shrank to half their original sizes.

The soldiers, warriors, men, and women were all kneeling.

For Snow.

His seven protectors remained standing, for which he was grateful. He was overwhelmed.

"Please rise." His voice wavered across the landscape, through the trees and budding copses of flowers, giving the forest stillness encasing their restless souls an optimistic depth.

"There are far more willing to fight for you," Doc said quietly to Snow. "They gather even now in all the villages and farms, in all the fields."

The figures surrounding them began to stand, resuming their tall forms.

Snow turned to Doc. "This is more people than you led me to believe."

"Yes."

Snow's heart bloomed at the single word answer. He had thought he had been forgotten. Not only presumed dead, but pronounced dead by the queen. And yet so many had not believed. Only a few of the queen's most loyal guards had known the truth. What had started to make people believe Snow still lived? Perhaps while drinking, men let truths slip out, or maybe because one or two still had a conscience they had told the secret to a few close friends, who in turn told their friends, and so on.

However it had happened, Snow was grateful. Humbled. Overcome with love for the land, the people, the entire realm.

Spurred on by such loyalty, now even more he wanted to fight. He knew deep inside Sleepy's worry and pain and anger that his lover understood this need.

Doc had been right. Sleepy was the most vulnerable of them all. Because he was in love. And because Snow was in love with him.

Snow reached for Sleepy's hand in the dark and found it. The skin was cool, the fingers slightly curled.

He fit his hand to Sleepy's, who at first did not respond. But gradually, the strong fingers closed fully about Snow's smaller hand, encasing it, giving it an encouraging squeeze.

The liquid heat of pleasure, of love, raced through Snow's entire body.

Snow looked up at him, but Sleepy did not turn his head. He was half-hidden by his brown hood.

"We re-group in another two miles and meet up with more of us. Then we stop at Gire's farm. He will have horses for some of us. But most of us will remain on foot."

Assenting voices rumbled through the forest.

"The plan is to reach the castle by dawn. We have friends outside and within."

Snow would have liked to know more about the plan. Details. But he had hours yet for the men to fill him in.

And for Sleepy to forgive him.

*

A hundred strong they walked. Sticks snapped. Rocks scattered under heavy boot steps. Even though it had rained the day before, dust flew up into a vaporous cloud around them.

Some of the throng conversed in low, secret tones. But most went quietly. A march to battle for what one believed in made many turn inward and contemplative. But still others could not contain their wildness. Their fury to defeat the enemy lit their hearts and blood on fire.

Snow understood both kinds of people. He felt antsy and philosophical at the same time. If he was to die tonight, it would be for a reason. Not some senseless assassination by the old lady where his bones were crunched by wild animals.

The thought of losing Sleepy made his stomach knot. But Sleepy was strong. If anyone were to survive this, even in the worst scenario, it would be Sleepy.

Snow wanted to tell him how proud he was of him. How grateful.

He didn't have the words.

Finally, he found his voice. "Sleepy."

The man trudged along beside him, all browns and dark honeyed hues from the swaying lanterns. Their hands had dropped, no longer connecting.

"Hm?"

"Thank you for everything."

"Don't thank me. We haven't saved you yet." Resigned. An edge of bitter rue.

"I'm remembering everything you said to me. Every single word."

"Every word I ever said?" Sleepy huffed.

Snow wanted to take Sleepy in his arms. Go back to the weeks before the cat escaped, before he'd been poisoned. To the quietude of keeping house. To looking forward to every night, to being in bed with Sleepy in his arms.

"Yes."

"Sometimes I speak before I think things through."

"I mean I remember every word of what you said to me yesterday. The things you meant to say."

Silence.

Snow took a deep breath. "No matter what happens—" Another breath. "I want you to name every flower you see after me."

He heard Sleepy clear his throat.

"I want you to look at the moon and see my soul. I want you to tell me all the funny stories you have ever heard. I want you to memorize me. Yes. All of it. But most of all, I want *you* to survive. No matter what happens, tell me you will survive. And remember me. Keep my name on your lips and in your heart. And I will do the same."

Sleepy did not answer.

"Please. We are fighting for something we believe in. I know that. But we are fighting for each other, too. Both of us. No matter what form the future takes, promise me we will always fight for each other. Always. Even if only the memory remains."

"Don't speak like that." Voice low and trembling.

"That's why I'm speaking like this. We both have to have a reason to fight harder today, to stay alive. You're mine, Sleepy. First and foremost. Let me be yours."

"You *are* mine!"

"But you have no faith in me."

"I do!"

"I am no longer Snow to you now. I can hear it in your voice. I'm the arrogant prince who has no sense, who's been locked away and is weak and still thinks he can win a fight against another powerful force. I'm the figurehead around which the rebels rally. But really, I am strong now. Because of you. I'm just a man, yes. But a man in love with you. It makes me feel real for the first time. And all I really want is you. To be together. The rest is like a dream, but you're my reality. You are Benjamin, the man who has made me whole."

Something like an anguished cry escaped Sleepy's mouth.

Snow felt a hand reach out and grab him by the upper arm, and pull him from the line of men. Sneezy, Bash and Doc turned to look, but let them go. Kept walking.

Sleepy pulled Snow to the side and under a low-branched tree.

The swaying lanterns held by some of the men faded down the line, but Snow could still see the beautiful planes and firm lines of Sleepy's face, the down-turned eyes and brow, the quivering of his lower lip. Wispy curves of shiny brown hair escaped the cloak's hood.

Snow raised his hands and cupped Sleepy's cheeks.

"Look at me," Snow said.

Sleepy's eyelids rose. His dark gaze met Snow's.

"We are in this together. No matter what."

Sleepy's throat flexed as he swallowed hard.

"No matter what," Snow repeated.

Finally, his lips parted. His mouth opened. "I—I—" Eyes blinking unshed tears. "—don't think you're arrogant."

Snow smiled. A laugh bubbled up inside him. His hands went to the back of Sleepy's neck, pulling him down toward him.

Their kiss was like a nectar he'd long craved, and would never get enough of.

Chapter Twenty-Three

The sky turned purple above them. The trees had thinned and they came to the edge of the forest.

Before them the plains of farmland stretched far as the eye could see. Little ponds flashed like spilled coins of silver here and there. To the north, on a white hill overlooking it all, stood the gleaming palace in shades of ivory and gold.

The clouds over the palace had a green tinge. The sun had not yet come up, but a rosy haze flooded the low, eastern part of the plain.

They stood in the hundreds now. Perhaps a thousand.

The rebels who had stolen through the blackness of the night poised still and silent, looking at the beauty stretched out before them, and the home of the evil that had threatened their land for ten long years. A few were on horseback. The occasional sputtering breaths of the horses broke the silence.

Snow was front and center of the army, his hood off and bunched about his shoulders, his pale hair exposed for all to see. Sleepy stood at his back, a warm, strong presence.

As if some invisible signal had been sent or seen, a shadow fell upon the land just beyond the palace along the left side of the white hill. It encroached upon the palace, growing.

Men on horseback. Guards on foot. Armed. Armored in leather and steel.

"The queen has been warned!" Someone yelled out.

"As we knew she would be. We have our agents in their ranks, and I'm sure they have theirs in our ranks."

The shadow formed into a broad, dark line in front of the palace.

This was the border they were to cross. The line of the queen's defenders.

"We are not equal in number," someone else pointed out.

"We are," Doc said quietly.

It finally dawned on Snow that Doc was the ring-leader. At least in the higher mountain regions. Snow had not actually put two and two together until now.

Doc followed up his reassuring answer by lifting his arm and pointing to the west.

In the brown night shadows of the land, flashes of light, a cloud of dust. Men were riding. A lot of men. Maybe five hundred. They headed straight for the palace and the army that now surrounded it.

"We will approach but not yet."

Doc's order was translated to the back of the ranks.

"We wait until the first surge. Then we make our run down the side of this slope. They haven't seen us yet. But by the time they do, they will be surrounded."

Only hours ago, Snow had thought this was a tiny operation made up of farmhands and miners and unorganized gangs. He had pictured a few scarred and angry men, or disgruntled shopkeepers afraid of higher taxes.

But the old lady had hurt scores of people on levels greater than that of stealing their earnings. She had maimed, poisoned, scarred and murdered.

Snow was only her more famous victim.

His energy surged. Tears of gratitude as well as grief filmed his vision.

On Doc's mark, they began their trek downward. Rapid but organized. Apparently, to Snow's perception, they had some training. No one pushed or shoved. They did not try to pass each other or fall back.

The noise and the dust propelled them onward.

When they arrived at flatter ground, Doc and Bash, Hap and Sneezy began to organize the men further into units.

The units began to surround Snow while pressing forward.

As their prince, Snow had been told they would form a wall to either side of him. They would all do their best to protect them. The guilt of that behavior, as if his life was worth more than theirs, would haunt Snow to the end of his days.

Sleepy was now one step ahead of Snow.

All swords remained sheathed.

Trying to stay clear-headed and determined, Snow focused on putting one foot in front of the other.

No one spoke except the men giving orders to maintain pace and direction.

Snow could not see Doc. Hap was two paces to the side of Sleepy, moving steadily, head held high.

Snow allowed his thoughts to wander to his weeks in the cave. In their precious, underhill home.

When the units on either side of him entered the fray, and the sounds of swords unsheathed and metal swinging against metal rang through the air, Snow did not think. He reacted.

He unsheathed his sword and moved along with the walls of men cutting a path to the palace.

In his mind, he saw the hearth burning to low, orange embers, and Sil was sitting on the long, wooden table, her green eyes glowing, with the house all to herself. In regal posture, she waited for her men to come home.

As his vision unfurled, his body automatically posed. All his training as a teenager for five years before the queen put a stop to it had returned.

His sword master had always told him: *Pick a reason, and fight for it. Focus on that. Nothing else. Fight for it because it is precious, it is yours, and you cannot ever allow it to be taken from you. Then, and only then, will you succeed even if you are not the finest swordsmen in the group.*

Sleepy. Peace. Family. Hearth. Home waited for Snow in some near-future as he saw an enemy man slip through their front line and advance.

Snow's sword hit the other's without him really seeing it swing. He impaled the man's arm, forcing him back before another man quickly turned and finished him off.

Snow saw the spray of blood but refused to acknowledge it. It was too much to comprehend, that human life would be snuffed so easily, so quickly. And that it would be many who died on this field today.

He was much happier focusing on Sil waiting for them to return, and letting his hind-brain instincts take over.

He was safe for the moment as Sleepy took down another man who broke through their ranks.

Protecting the prince was top priority, but Snow fought forward, sword raised, and cut down another man which Sleepy finished off.

This went on for a period of time Snow could not track. Maybe it was minutes. Or hours. He wasn't sure.

During that time he watched Sleepy dispatch enemy after enemy as if it was no effort for him, as if he was merely on an evening stroll, Snow following in his boot prints. He thought again of the cat. Was she hungry? Had they remembered to leave her food and water?

These quiet ministrations of his mind kept him calm. Love gave him a reason to push. He had built bonds with the cat and all the men. He was determined to see this through.

He barely noticed when his sword went straight through the throat of an enemy about to attack Sleepy from the side.

Sleepy turned to see what he'd done, eyes wide. Then he gave Snow a gracious nod and pushed forward into more chaos, more shadows.

Snow hurried forward. His wall of men moved with him, always forward, the path open so he could make his way to his old home. His rightful throne.

He walked over broken bodies and puddles of blood.

For every dead man his soul broke off a piece of itself and tumbled away.

Some time had passed, Snow could see, for dawn had painted a blood red sun against a candy pink sky. It was majestic and magical, oblivious to the stench of death below.

There had been a constant rumble for what seemed like hours. Snow had thought it was his own breathing. His heart. But it was the mingled shouts and yells of the men, the steps on the ground which literally shook beneath them. All of it making a sound on the edge of reality that shouldn't exist but did because humans had hold of the script.

Snow moved as if in a dream where he could not wake. Where his feet got stuck in mud, except this mud was red. This mud was blood.

His eyes were dry though he wanted to weep.

Sleepy neatly danced his way through the enemy lines, a single force no one could contend with.

Briefly, Snow got glimpses of Bash and Doc, fighting back to back. They were swift with their swords, surprisingly seasoned as warriors.

When had they all had the time to practice? The quarry?

Though they had revealed their souls to Snow, these men he'd lived with for many weeks had hidden talents. Snow was amazed.

Suddenly, a cry went through the air, higher than the perpetual low rumble. The forces in front broke way.

Five men ambushed Sleepy and he went down beneath them, metal flashing.

"Sleepy, no!" Snow rushed forward.

His mind went black. He could feel his arm raising and lowering over and over, the impacts jerking him nearly off his feet.

When the dust cleared, when he could see again, Sleepy lay on the ground surrounded by bodies.

Doc and Bash had come running but too late. The men were dead. Snow had taken them all. They looked at him in surprise.

Snow stared at Sleepy, who lay on his side, shirt torn at the shoulder, unmoving.

Snow yelled, then howled, a cry going up into the air like a final command.

Men scattered.

"They're retreating!" Someone yelled.

Sleepy moved.

Snow bent down.

Sleepy raised his head. Then his hand.

Snow took it and pulled him up to stand.

Doc and Bash came forward but Snow would not let them touch Sleepy. He had to know for himself. He touched him everywhere, all over, looking for blood, looking for wounds. He counted all his limbs. Everything was intact.

Sleepy merely raised an eyebrow and said, "I will never doubt your expertise with a sword again."

Someone ran up to Doc. "They're retreating! The Queen's Guard is retreating. We have the palace!"

The ranks parted all down the field and to the white hill where the palace rose in reflected glory of the now late dawn.

The white marble columns reflected pink. The tower where Snow had been imprisoned gleamed, gold-tipped. Yellow banners whipped in an early summer wind.

The gate before them was open. The rebels lined themselves up against it, as if to salute their prince as he passed, as well as guard him from any surviving, errant assassin.

A winding path, lined with little violet and blue flowers, led up and up, past landings with gardens and benches, past patches of mud as they walked higher, past a giant apple orchard on the side of the hill east of the palace.

As they approached the palace steps and landing, more men lined up in rows, creating a narrower and narrower path until all Snow could see was something white on the marble landing.

It was the old lady. Queen Serena was on her knees, held fast by two rebel swordsmen.

She was alive.

Immediately upon seeing this spectacle, Sleepy took Snow's hand in his own. He knew Doc and Bash, Hap and Dope, Sneezy and Grump were right behind him. Fortified with their strength, still Snow's stomach clenched and his body began to tremble upon seeing her.

He tasted the bitter remains of poisoned apple still deep in his throat.

Even on her knees, Queen Serena looked fresh as a new bloom, lily petal soft, her golden hair piled high and shining on the top of her head. Her white gown was spotless, decorated with a gold belt. She wore a choker with a ruby stone. Her arms jangled with bracelets.

Everything about her looked pure, clean, rich, beautiful, except the eyes which gazed up through madness and hatred as Snow approached.

Her first words to him were, "You think you're better than I. Stronger. Smarter. More beautiful."

Snow shook his head.

"It is I who ruled these past ten years. I know the ways, the land and the kingdom. You are nothing but a boy."

"Not anymore, he's not," said Doc, stepping forward.

"Tate." She spat the word, her lower lip trembling.

"Serena."

Snow turned to look at Doc. They knew each other?

"You always were a little snipe, brother!"

"And you were spoiled rotten because of your beauty. I could never get you to stop looking in mirrors."

"And look what gazing into mirrors got me! I made a king fall for me. And then I became a queen."

"Yes. But to keep your power, you stooped too low. And here I am now."

"You did this!" she cried out.

Doc nodded. "Someone had to. I knew you too well. I knew the things you were capable of even when we were kids. Hurting animals. Bullying the children of the other servants. We had a good life, wealthy, well-educated, but you made it ugly. And you took your ugliness and spread it to the land and innocent people. I knew you, sister. Too well. And I knew some day I would make you stop."

Serena jerked in the arms of the men holding her down. "You spiteful traitor! You're jealous. Of me! That's all it is."

The old lady—Doc's sister--turned a cold dark gaze on Snow. "Snow, darling, you're looking well. Can we let bygones be bygones? For surely you can see what this man is. What he's done. He's a murderer, you know. Tortured two helpless men to death!"

"I know Doc quite well," Snow replied coolly. "He's a good man."

"He's not and I have proof. Just let me speak. Let me show you. We can come to a truce, you and I, as soon as you order him and his men away."

She was mad. Something inside her had broken long ago beyond repair. She acted sane at times, even rational if cruel, but she was not sane. And her appetite was evil.

Snow had experienced it first hand. And apparently, Doc had known her even longer. Siblings. She had called Doc *little brother,* but they looked of an age. They couldn't be more than a year apart. Nearly twins.

"I will not order them away," Snow said. He surprised himself with how calm he was as he spoke to her. "Doc—uh—Tate is my good friend. And you, Serena, must be held accountable for your crimes."

"My crimes?" She laughed long and loud.

"False imprisonment, rape and murder just to name a few of the worst. Ordering your guards to do your dirty work. Thieving, pillaging, killing when it suited them."

She grunted, face twisting in a sort of pain as he fought her imprisonment by the men holding her. "You thought it was rape what I did to you? Ah, little boy, you were the luckiest of males to be with the most beautiful, the fairest in all the land. You remember that you ungrateful imp. You remember!"

Snow drew himself up. He wasn't a little boy any longer.

"For your crimes, the punishment is death." He spoke clearly. Not loud. Not proud. But he was heard. It was his duty to be fair. To give justice to the realm once and for all. She could not be allowed to live.

"When would you like us to carry out the sentence, my lord? Uh, Your Highness," asked one of the men holding Serena.

Snow took a breath and let it slowly out. "I do not want her to suffer. Now will not be soon enough."

"The sword, Your Highness?"

Snow nodded.

Queen Serena began to scream.

Doc said nothing. Snow could not meet his eyes.

As the old lady was dragged away to the courtyard to the chopping block, a thing Snow's father had never used, but she had used a hundred times, Snow turned away.

He should probably watch. He was about to be made king. But he couldn't. More blood would run this day. Hers. It was earned and justified, but still too much.

Snow listened as her screams rang upon the air. Then they stopped, and he knew the deed had been done, quick and merciful. A roar of celebration came up from all who had fought on the hill and beyond.

The palace of the White Hills belonged to Snow now.

Sleepy came up behind him, a solid, pressing warmth.

Snow turned into him.

"Can we go home now?"

Epilogue

Yellow forsythia. Bobbing bluebonnets. Red snapdragons. Jack-in-the-Pulpit whose poison properties hid behind a veneer of beauty.

Crabapple. White maple. Thorn and rowan. Oak and alder. Trees so green they filled the gaze with nothing but their greenness.

Here in the White Hills the landscape was a nymph-wood, an elfin forest in summer so breathtaking that Snow's heart wanted to burst from his body. He could walk it any time he wanted now, safe and secure. Knowing he was home.

Today was brisk but warm, and Sleepy walked beside Snow, his white shirt billowing at the sleeves, his dark hair loose and wavy.

They sauntered along Leafbrook stream, not far from the underground abode Snow would always think of as home.

He had to come back right away. He had to. He could not say goodbye yet to the woods or the lovely bed he shared with Sleepy, or any of it. To the hearth that burned so sweet. To the leaking roof and the pans that caught the drips. To the long table, the clever cupboards and shelves, the hand woven floor rugs that kept down the dust. Simply, he did not want to leave that shadowed house.

Plus, they could not leave Sil. Of course Doc would want her in the palace. As would they all.

Doc, Bash, Sneezy, Grump, Hap and Dope all stayed behind to organize the troops. They sent most of them home, and paid them from the palace treasury for their contribution. The ones who needed jobs they hired on as the king's guard.

Snow wondered how long it would take him to break the habit of calling them all by their nicknames. He knew their real names now, after they'd all knelt to him and officially pledged themselves to their new king only yesterday.

Doc was Tate. He had never told a soul Serena was his sister until she'd been overthrown. Not even Bash. Until the day of her execution.

Doc's lover, Bash, was Robin. Hap's real name was Sterling. Grump was John, and Sneezy, Derrick. Last but not least, the youngest of the bunch, Dope, had been born Michael.

As a king now, Snow had immediately knighted them all. Made them his own on every level he could think of, official and personal. They were his most trusted right hands. They were his family.

After a lot of wine, and some rum, and a celebratory feast, Sleepy granted Snow's wish to be taken home.

What a long day it had been!

But he still did not want to wait. He wanted to be home.

The others complained that having Sleepy as Snow's only personal guard on this trip would not be enough. There might be rogues who'd been in league with the queen left behind, still wandering the woods. They offered to come along.

But Snow insisted they would be fine. Their trip back would be a secret. Plus, he wanted alone-time with Sleepy. With Benjamin.

Doc, as the king's official first right hand, said he would hold off any official coronation ceremonies and appearances until Snow was ready to receive his public.

Sleepy and Snow had taken two fine horses and ridden off into the night.

When they had arrived at the little house, they took a short nap, but Snow was too excited to sleep.

He wanted to walk the woods. He wanted to embrace his true freedom in the White Hills, the land he called home.

So now they walked, Leafbrook chattering happily before them, the sparrows darting from tree branch to tree branch, chirping. It had been a sparrow who had helped Snow keep his sanity in the prison tower. From bread crumbs on a window sill to this—he'd come a long way.

Butterflies flitted before them. Sleepy was smiling all the time now. His gorgeous mouth, his white teeth, his tender flashing brown eyes.

Though the creek was cold, they bathed in it, teeth chattering, arms around each other as the water flowed past their thighs. They kissed but that was all.

When they returned to their underground home, they made a quick supper, fed the cat, and climbed tiredly back into bed.

Snow rolled easily into Sleepy's arms, fitting their bodies together. Sleepy's skin was scented with summer wind, and the cool stream.

Snow felt Sleepy's arousal against his thigh and wanted to make love. But he was so tired. Instead, he fell asleep dreaming of making love.

Abruptly, he woke in the dark, thinking he'd been dreaming of the old lady. But he could not remember.

For a moment, he thought he was lost in the woods with the huntsman.

He remembered the truth and reached for Sleepy, all solid and blanket-warmed.

Sleepy reached back. Rolled him with his weight. Head up now and looking down at him, face revealed by a sheaf of light from the hearth, Sleepy cupped one side of Snow's face.

Snow's body thrummed at the sweet touch. His skin began to burn. His cock filled.

Sleepy said, "My king. I am at your command."

Snow snorted, and burst into a laugh. "Don't call me that in bed." He inhaled sharply. "Unless it turns you on."

"*You* turn me on."

Snow tightened his arms around Sleepy's shoulders and tugged at him. Their lips met, velvet soft, warm as a sun-filled glade in May.

They grew hot under the covers as the kiss deepened.

Sleepy threw back the light-weight, summer blankets, lifted himself and sat back.

Snow's gaze traced his body, the grace of it, the poise in how he held his shoulders, chin turned slightly to one side, bangs flopped over the left eye, waist narrowing to trim hips, cock lifted by its own excitement and Sleepy's unabashed love for Snow. It pointed upward from the shadows between his legs.

Sleepy's arms bulged, the curved biceps flexing, as he ran his hands from Snow's face to his chest, rubbing lightly. Snow rested his palms on Sleepy's arms, like chiseled polished rock. He was like a sculpture you could not stop looking at. A satyr. A god.

When Sleepy's caresses moved lower and reached Snow's aching cock, he took it gently in hand and began to stroke.

Snow's knees bent in pleasure. His thighs pressed hard at Sleepy kneeling between his legs.

Sleepy's brown-tousled head lowered and he licked the tip.

They were alone for the first time and Snow felt less inhibited. He was free now on so many levels.

He let out a loud moan that might also have been a shout. It echoed off the stone walls, sounding louder than it probably was.

Sleepy took the head into his mouth and gently sucked.

Snow's fists gripped the sheets until he thought they might tear.

When Sleepy became more exuberant, taking him all the way into his mouth, grasping his hips and sliding his hands underneath to knead his buttocks, Snow almost came.

He pushed himself up on his elbows. "I love it, oh, I do. But wait. I want us to take our time. I want—I want—"

The hot mouth and dancing tongue sucked up, then off, leaving Snow's cock damp and naked, bobbing eagerly.

"What do you want?"

"I—I want what you talked to me about once, but then you never brought it up again. How men connect—even deeper. Physically, I mean."

A grin flashed across Sleepy's face, white and amused, but he quickly suppressed it.

Snow could tell Sleepy was trying not to laugh, and his face heated. "If you don't want it, want me to—" He gulped.

Strong hands ran up Snow's waist to his chest again. Sleepy leaned down. "Oh, I want it. But do you know what you are saying?"

Snow blinked, then turned his face into the pillow, half-embarrassed, but even more turned on at the thought of Sleepy teaching him something more intimate than they'd already done. "Show me."

Immediately, Sleepy slid from the bed and strode to the cupboards by the hearth.

"Sleepy? Where are you going?" Snow rolled to his side, propping himself on his elbow.

No answer.

"Are you abandoning me? Are you upset?" He asked jokingly, for he knew it wasn't true.

Sleepy returned to the side of the bed, handsome cock swinging, naked and gleaming. He had a small glass jar in his hand.

"I would never abandon you," he said, setting the jar by Snow's free hand.

"What is it?" But he knew. A slick oil would be needed to make the joining more comfortable.

He knew that much from his unfortunate past with the old lady, who sometimes lathered him up so she could ride him for hours at her whim.

He didn't want that. Didn't want Sleepy to ride him. He looked up as Sleepy got back into bed and rolled him onto his back. He straddled Snow's hips.

"You in me," Snow said softly, pushing at Sleepy's hips so he could spread his legs and get him between them again.

Sleepy looked at him. "So you know what you're asking."

"I have an idea. Show me more. Everything."

Sleepy's grin lit up the room. "First you need to lie back, get comfortable and just relax."

Snow scooted back in the bed until he could wrap his legs around Sleepy's waist. He bit at his own smile. "Like this?"

Sleepy frowned though his eyes were still smiling. "Hmm. I think you know more than you are saying."

"I don't. I want you to talk me through it."

For once, Sleepy looked almost embarrassed. It was quite becoming. "I will do my very best."

Snow laughed as Sleepy swooped over him, gathered him into his arms and kissed him.

Always, the kissing set Snow on fire. Things heated up even more when Sleepy moved his mouth to Snow's neck and chest. He kissed him everywhere, over and over until Snow arched in desire.

Sleepy's strong hands ran all up and down his sides, arms, chest and between Snow's legs. Snow's groans filled the room.

Sleepy sure knew how to stretch out the anticipation.

Gently, finally, Sleepy slipped his fingers underneath Snow and teased his crack.

Snow wanted every touch and this was what he'd been waiting for. He bent his knees to give him more access.

"All right?" Sleepy asked.

"Oh yes." Everywhere Sleepy touched was more than *all right.*

182

Sleepy paused to grab the small bottle he'd brought to their bed. Snow watched him pour a generous amount of oil into his palm, then slip his hand beneath Snow again.

Gentle fingers probed.

Sleepy leaned down and kissed him on the mouth. "Relax. It might be odd at first. Let me know if you want me to stop."

"No. Keep going." He was so aroused he wanted anything, everything.

A finger pushed its way into him. It wasn't too odd, but he did have to close his eyes and blank his mind so he could focus and feel. Get used to it.

Sleepy's kisses made everything work. All the touches, even the most intrusive and intimate, were welcome. Anything Sleepy wanted Sleepy could have as far as Snow was concerned, as long as Sleepy kept kissing him.

The finger caressed him, still gently, but began to move in and out of him in a rhythm Snow matched with his own hips beginning to move in need. This was like a dance, and he was learning quickly.

Sleepy said, "A little more. Another finger."

Snow nodded, suddenly breathless.

"You need to stretch a bit more. Gradual is more comfortable. Be patient and I will make it worth your while." He grinned. "I hope."

The second finger stretched him wider. He felt that. A little sting but nothing more. Sleepy pulled out, perhaps seeing his wince, and added more oil.

It wasn't long before Snow was moving his hips again, and moaning. For there was something within him that sent him into quick euphorias every time Sleepy brushed his fingers there.

He blurted out, "More."

"As I promised, there is pleasure there."

"Yes. Something—something you keep touching."

"I know. It's a little bump. Every man had one but most men never find out how much pleasure it can give."

"Show me more," Snow demanded.

Sleepy nodded. "I will." He kept his fingers busy for a while, pushing in and out, and his other hand gently petted Snow's cock where it lay hard and damp against his abdomen.

"You are so beautiful," Sleepy said. "You are doing so well."

The encouragement made Snow squirm with impatience. "Join with me. Do it. Please."

Laughing, Sleepy pulled his fingers free. He then oiled up his cock until it glistened. Snow loved the sight of him, his hard body, his arousal flaring strong with longing and love.

Softly, "Bend your knees a little more and pull them up. If this position is too difficult for you, you can turn over."

"No. I want to see your face." He wanted to view Sleepy's every reaction. The tender need in his eyes. He wanted their joining to be flesh as well as mind.

Snow bent his knees, put his hands against the backs of his thighs and pulled them up.

Sleepy gasped. Even in shadow, Sleepy would be able to see him, open and ready for him.

Snow's cock twitched at the thought.

With great care, Sleepy pressed himself against Snow, lining up his cock with Snow's entrance. He took his time, teasing, then pushed the head of his cock past the ring of muscle.

At first Snow thought it wouldn't give way. But then a burn and another push and Sleepy was in. Not all the way, but still he was inside him.

"Deep breaths," Sleepy whispered. "Oh, Snow. It's so good."

"More." Snow was ready. He could feel the oil allowing a smooth slide. It soothed even as the first entry had burned.

Snow bucked up a little.

Sleepy, hands on his hips, pressed him down. "Not too fast."

"You want more, too," Snow said.

"Yes, but not until you're ready."

"Push," Snow ordered, and he wrapped his hands around Sleepy's wrists at his hips, taking the weight off so he could buck up again.

"Oh. Hell." Sleepy's eyes shut tight and his lips tightened.

Snow felt the hard cock enter him deeper, pulsing hot. He wanted him all the way in, so he moved again and felt Sleepy's balls brush against him.

How full he was. Strangely wonderful and alluring. But he needed to get used to it.

"Can you—can you hold still for a minute?" Snow took a few deep breaths, watching Sleepy nod, the pleasure never leaving his face.

184

This was what Snow wanted to see, to watch, to do. He wanted them to be close, as close as possible. And he needed to see Sleepy's face in full-blown ecstasy.

It did not take long for Snow's body to adapt to the intruder—the welcome intruder. His lover.

His heart beat harder in his chest. His pulse thrummed. His cock throbbed with need.

"You can move now, please." Snow's voice came out soft, pleasure-thick.

Sleepy withdrew a fraction, and pushed forward.

"Again," Snow said.

This time the thrust was longer, deeper.

Snow pushed up to meet him. First awkward, but soon finding a cadence.

The cock inside him began to slide in and out as if it were the more natural thing, a dance of pure pleasure. As Snow and Sleepy built a rhythm, Sleepy cried out in pleasure over and over. His enthusiasm glowed on his cheeks, in his eyes. His cock began to rub and pulse against that bump inside Snow that sent him reeling.

This was pure joining now. This was making love.

One of Sleepy's hands took hold of Snow's cock and began to milk him. It was almost too much. The sensation within. The sensation without. Their voices mingled as they could not hold back their moans, their cries.

Snow reached up and grasped at Sleepy's shoulders to pull him closer.

Sleepy bent down, keeping up the rhythm, and removed his hand from Snow's cock and pulled him up and close. Snow was almost, but not quite sitting against his lap, his buttocks sliding up Sleepy's thighs. His cock slid against Sleepy's hard stomach.

Sleepy supported himself against the bed with one hand, so he could continue to thrust his hips back and forth, and with his other hand he cradled Snow against his chest.

"Oh, keep going. I'm almost—I'm going to—"

The sensation of his cock rubbing against hard muscle as well as the internal stimulation sent Snow right over the cliff and into ecstasy, riding Sleepy through an orgasm so deep and intense he thought he'd never recover.

He heard Sleepy yell and felt the warmth of his lover's orgasm fill him.

They clung together in pure amazement, sharing the fall, the whirl of love that overtook them.

Snow breathed hard against Sleepy's chest. Sleepy slowed his thrusts until they stilled altogether, but he was still inside him, warm, big.

Snow began to laugh. "That was—"

Sleepy joined in. "You are fantastic."

"Amazing."

"Stupendous."

"Fabulous."

Their laughter made them fall back together. Sleepy's cock slid out and already Snow missed him.

"Let's do it again," Snow said.

"Oh, never fear, young man. We will."

They dozed and made love two more times that night.

By morning they slept the sleep of contented and exhausted men.

The sun was already high in the sky by the time they rose. Sleepy stood naked by the fire warming up some soup.

Snow, also wearing nothing, came up alongside him. "Did you feed the cat?"

"Yes."

"How are you this morning?" Snow asked.

"Shouldn't I be asking that of you?"

Snow laughed. "I'm absolutely perfect." He put his hand on the side of Sleepy's face and kissed him. "I could stay here forever."

"We should go back to the palace soon," Sleepy said.

"Just one more day," Snow replied. "Please. One more day."

Sleepy's beautiful grin spread over his face.

The soon-to-be-king got his wish.

The End

Dear Reader:

Thank you for reading "Snow of the White Hills." I loved writing this book!

Please consider leaving a review. Word of mouth is like gold! If it weren't for the generous support of my readers, I could not be writing more books!

If you enjoyed this book, you might also enjoy subscribing to my newsletter. I put it out several times a year to announce new books and upcoming projects, and I always have sales and freebies to offer readers both from myself and other authors I enjoy reading. If you subscribe at the link below, you can get a free copy of my contemporary mm romance *Buying You.*

Or, if newsletters aren't your thing, it is very easy to sign up for my Facebook group Wendyland to keep up to date.

For new release notifications, it's also super easy to simply follow my author page on Amazon.

Happy Reading!

Love,

Wendy Rathbone

*

Contact links for Wendy Rathbone:

Join my Facebook group Wendyland. I post updates, cover reveals, snippets, sales and other fun stuff every day: https://www.facebook.com/groups/718074255203918/

Facebook: https://www.facebook.com/wendy.rathbone.3

Newsletter sign up (you get a free copy of my contemporary mm romance *Buying You*): https://claims.prolificworks.com/free/iE2sKi9b

Amazon author page: https://www.amazon.com/Wendy-Rathbone/e/B00B0O9BMS/ref=dp_byline_cont_ebooks_1

About Wendy Rathbone

I love to write.

The reason I write romance these days is because the overwhelming power of falling in love is a game-changer. It makes sad people instantly happy. It makes bleak reality look sun-warmed and friendly again.

I have written in all genres: sci-fi, fantasy, horror, paranormal, contemporary, erotica, romance. But I keep coming back to romance as the main focus. Gay romance. Male/male romance. The idea of two men falling in love is irresistible to me.

All my books are available on Amazon and most are in Kindle Unlimited. So if you have the urge, go take a look. See what's on the shelf.

Love to you all!
Wendy Rathbone

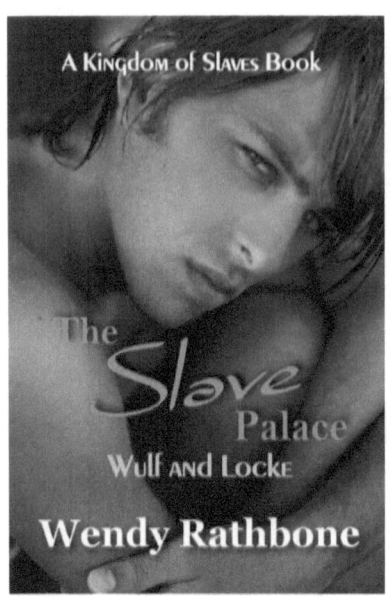

THE SLAVE PALACE
Wulf and Locke

WENDY RATHBONE

Conquered. Captured. Sold as a pleasure slave.

After being taken as a prisoner of war, Wulf fights his captors and is sold as a One-Night Thrall to be used and abused, then put to death. He is purchased by a high ranking master of the famous Slave Palace. Why Locke buys him, Wulf has no clue, but something about this master is intriguing. Instead of abuse, Wulf is plied with luxuries he has never known by a man who actually seems to respect him.

Jaded. Looking for a challenge.

Eminent Master Locke takes on a bet with his best friend that he can't train and tame a dangerous One-Night Thrall in ten days. But something about this slave stirs him like no other before. All bets aside, Locke has the urge to keep Wulf, as well as save his life. But Wulf is fierce, unwilling, and his consent papers have been forged. If Wulf doesn't soon submit to his role as a slave, he will be sent to death as a prisoner of war.

A sweet, slow-burn love story taking place on an alternate contemporary Earth where owning pleasure slaves is legal.

LORD VAMPYRE
Wendy Rathbone

When Lord Neverelle becomes a guest at Cliffside Keep, Vanni watches helplessly as Damion, the young man he's grown up with and secretly loves, falls for the alluring and seductive stranger. Lord Neverelle is danger incarnate, and soon takes control of the household.

Not satisfied with Damion alone, Never uses a vampire trick called "the tempt" to compel Vanni, who is swept into a love triangle that includes fiery passion and nightly threesomes.

Now Vanni must ask himself, is any of this consensual? And what about Damion—does he really want to be with Vanni, or is it all a sensual play controlled by vampire compulsion?

M/M and M/M/M romance.

THE IMPOSTER KING
(Book 2 of The Imposter Series)
Wendy Rathbone

Their love made them close. Their secret kept them closer.

Dare and Prince Malory are happily married and in love, but the secret of Dare's true identity as a mere servant threatens their romantic bliss.

Messages to the king of Brookfall go unanswered, and rumors of war unsettle both kingdoms. Until one day heralds arrive with bags of gold to ransom Dare and demand his return to Brookfall.

King Millard, Prince Malory's father, orders Dare to make the journey to see his father. But Dare is not the true heir, and if they meet, the secret he and Mal have been guarding will be revealed. Also, impersonating a royal means a death penalty offense. Worse, it could mean all-out war between their countries.

Panic. Despair. Lovers torn asunder. Personal sacrifice. More dark secrets revealed. An ending that will leave you breathless.

The Imposter Prince
Book 1 in The Imposter Series
Wendy Rathbone

His love for an enemy prince threatens his very life.

Dare does not mind serving the spoiled and cruel Prince Darius. Growing up with him, Dare does everything for Darius including homework, bed play demands, and even doubling for him as the prince grows too paranoid to face even the smallest of crowds.

But everything changes in a single moment when Dare, while posing as Darius, is abducted by the enemy.

A captive in a new and hostile land, Dare meets another prince who seems just as indulged and rotten as Darius—until Dare gets to know him, until they fall in love. Against his will, Dare must continue to play the role of Prince Darius for real, or risk everything: his love, his land, and his very life.

His only chance for survival is to keep a secret from the one he loves, a secret that is also killing him.

A male/male, enemies to lovers novel of mad kings, troubled princes, abduction, fevers, cold dungeons, warm hearths, comfort, wine, and true love.

Ganymede: Abducted by the Gods
Book 1 in "The Fantastic Immortals" Series (A standalone read)
Wendy Rathbone

My name is Ganymede, and I have been betrayed.

Every boy my age dreams of leaving home to embark on a noble adventure, but never does any boy imagine it happening as it did to me. On the evening of my 18th naming day, when I expected no more than a chalice of wine and a few drunken flirtations to tempt my innocence, I was instead sold by my father to the god, Zeus - not because of anything particular I had ever done or said, but solely because I am considered beautiful among mortals, and my father found more value in a few gold coins than in the well-being of his youngest son.

To be honest, I never believed in the gods, but my lack of belief held no power in Olympus or on Earth. Now under Zeus's influence, I am kept drunk on ambrosia in the sun-lit halls of the immortals, alternately amazed and horrified at the power these beings hold over others, and how darkly they influence the progress of humanity itself. How very much I want to hate Zeus for kidnapping me, and yet he shows me mostly kindness, even on that fateful night when we shared a bed for the first time. Kindness, yes, but also a godly and unyielding refusal to take no for an answer... probably because he could read my ambrosia-fevered curiosity as much as my naive, inexperienced terror. He owns me, after all, just as he owns everything else, so perhaps it never occurred to him that a captive and a slave might not make the best of lovers.

Throughout my time at Olympus - who's to say how long I've been here, for time on Olympus is not the same as that on Earth - the only thing that gives me hope comes to me in dreams and visions. His name is Sable and he is a magnificent shape-shifter in the form of a giant raven. When he first spoke to me in my mind it was with a resonance unlike any I had ever known - his mind and mine sounding a single note together, a song without words, a promise of freedom, a glimpse of some distant but very real possibility of this thing we humans call Love. But now he is silent. Perhaps I dreamed his voice. Perhaps I have finally lost my mind.

ZEUS (Conquering His Heart)
Book 2 in "The Fantastic Immortals" Series (A standalone read)
WENDY RATHBONE

When I throw the lightning and summon the thunder, it isn't always out of anger, but often from a love so all-consuming it could only be the effect of Eros himself. Yes, he is beautiful. Of course he is. How could he be otherwise, with hair the color of sunlight and white-feathered wings that drape to the floor? And he is as ancient as the myth of time itself, an immortal with powers and glamour beyond my ability to imagine. He struggles to teach me wisdom, control, strategy, yet I sit here babbling like a child, for all I can think of is how I might try - at least let me try! - to prove myself to him in some way that will cause him to crave my company and my touch, just as I crave his.

I do not yet know how to be a god, for I am only 18 and still just a silly boy who has fallen in love with Love himself, while my father Cronus plots and schemes to lock me in his dungeon and make me his slave forever.

A male/male romance.

BUYING YOU
Wendy Rathbone

It's one thing to be a beautiful cover model on billboards, buses and magazine covers. It's quite another to be sold as one.

Prized for his looks, Dane knows it's shallow, but he is on his way to having it all. It feels good to be gorgeous, smart and have top designers from around the world requesting him.

When he returns to his hometown to participate in a small Date-For-Charity auction, it seems harmless enough—until a hooded man walks in and bids higher on him than anyone else. Dane is intrigued but nervous when he finds out the guy has vanished after the winning bid, leaving only a limo behind to whisk Dane off into the night.

Enemies to lovers, opposites attract, and hot steamy nights that challenge two guys' trust issues along with their biggest fears.

PREY
Wendy Rathbone

When the rescued slaves were first brought on board my ship, I saw only the one. The one they called Arcana. And though I realized the others had all suffered similar fates - fearsome torture and erotic conditioning that had estranged them from whoever they had once been - I focused on the one who met my eyes with what could only be interpreted as a defiantly seductive lure, while the others held their gazes downward, at their feet, at the floor, at the past which had shaped them and undoubtedly doomed them to any sort of normal life.

Not so with Arcana. That one had no shame in whatever had happened to him. In that one blinding moment when we saw one another for the first time, I knew he was as brash as he was beautiful, and I knew without any doubt that he had chosen me - though for what dark agenda, I could not have said.

My heart went cold and silent in my chest. My throat was dry. My breathing faltered and I was forever changed.

***

We danced. Captain Mordecai and I. Not any traditional dance, but a dance of power. A battle of yin and yang, light and dark, pleasure and torment. A dangerous dance of right and wrong in a single moment caught outside the tendrils of Time.

It was easy to see the raw and sensual power in that man's gaze. But also the fear. Fear of being seen for who he was behind his carefully-constructed masks. Fear of finally surrendering to the dangerous desires he clearly felt when he looked at me, knowing my past, knowing I had been enslaved by sadistic aliens. Knowing I had not only enjoyed it, but had come to love my master. All the wrong things. So very wrong.

That was when I knew he wanted me. That was when I knew I needed him.

That was when I knew I had him exactly where we both needed him to be.

LETTERS TO AN ANDROID
Wendy Rathbone

Cobalt is a created human, vat grown and born adult, with no human rights and indentured to serve others for the duration of his life. Liyan is a young man with wanderlust in his eyes, embarking on a career that takes him to the furthest regions of space. The two become unlikely friends and create a memorable long-distance correspondence. Through Liyan, Cobalt gets to explore the universe, living vicariously through his friend's wave transmissions. A strong bond develops between them that not even the stars can put asunder.

Now you know an android who writes poetry.

This is all your fault. Did you not read my last wave telling you extracurricular activities for my kind are discouraged? Of course this is harmless and strangely enjoyable and does not necessarily require me to leave the hotel. Pel would not care if I wrote lines of equations or nonsensical juxtaposed words. As long as the act does not bring my mental state into question.

However, in history, poetry is often written by the rebels.

So we can keep this to ourselves.

Let me know about your lieutenant's test.

And to give you peace of mind, I never believed you observed me as anything other than human.

Some people are and always will be hateful bigots. Most people are simply uncomfortable in speaking to "property." And anyway, friendship, like poetry, is also discouraged.

Your friend,

Cobalt

SONS OF NEVERLAND
Della Van Hise

"The virtuosity shown here is only the beginning of a pyrotechnic talent unfolding into the hidden dimensions of the human and nonhuman spirit."
-Jacqueline Lichtenberg

Set against a backdrop of contemporary culture, *Sons of Neverland* explores the universal questions of love, sex and death - the three most crucial challenges every human being must face. Stefan London is a grieving man, suffering through the loss of his young daughter. When he goes to a science fiction convention in the hopes of meeting her friends, he encounters instead a young man who is dangerously seductive and undeniably magical. Lured into the night, Stefan soon discovers himself in a place where vampires are real, and the world is not at all what he has always believed, and immortality is only a deep red kiss away.

But the price of eternal life is high, and as his handsome maker warns, "Through my blood you will learn a secret which will compel you to live forever, yet a secret so sinister it will haunt you for that same eternity."

The secret will haunt you, too.

———

"This book zones on the question of immortality. However, this is not just the decadent historical immortality of the long-lived vampire, it is immortality as a change in one's perception. This is the story behind the story, delivered by characters that are hyper-real - each one loaded with symbolism. *Sons of Neverland* will have you filled, even brimming over with the sense of Mysterium Tremendum et Fascinans. Go there for a full helping of the numinous." (A Reviewer on Amazon)

*Also available in paperback on Amazon,
or order from your favorite bookseller.*

Prince of Umberlight
Alexis Fegan Black

"If Prince of Umberlight doesn't rattle your cage, you're more dead than the undead!"
-Night Readers

Thorn may be an 800 year old vampire, but he does not possess the ability to create others of his kind, and so he is cursed to fall in love with mortals, only to watch them grow old and die. Torn by grief, Thorn denounces his immortality and enters into a comatose oblivion for decades.

When he awakens, he is no longer in London, but finds himself in a world spun into being by his own desires - a world where Time and Death do not exist, a world where it is forever autumn, where the Parish of Shadows and the River of Stars become his home. It is in this world of Umberlight that he meets Atom - an interloper into his private sanctuary, but also an impudent imp who is destined to reveal to Thorn the three dangerous elements a vampire must possess in order to become a Creator.

The Art of Brutality.
Submission to Dark Desire.
Love.

YEAR OF THE RAM
Della Van Hise

Year of the Ram was described by one reviewer as... "A space-faring male/male romance full of love, angst, and longing."

Only after Star Commander Morgan Diego becomes an exile as a result of a Galaxy Corps political blunder does he begin to realize how much he valued the companionship of his second in command - the mysterious Lucien, an Alfarian who is more elven than human, with peculiar powers & abilities which begin to unfold as he, too, realizes what he has lost.

Separated by circumstance from his former life, Morgan is thrust into a world where he must survive by his wits. When he meets a peculiar little old man calling himself Kim Le, Morgan finds himself in a situation where he is required to master The Art - not only a form of human & extraterrestrial martial arts, but a way of living and being that will alter his life forever.

At the temple, he is introduced to his new teacher, another Alfarian who begins to steal his heart - a heart which is already promised to Lucien. Torn and conflicted, Morgan struggles with the world he left behind and the world he now inhabits.

Beginning to believe he may never again return to his ship and to the friends and loved ones he left behind, he is all the more frustrated and heartbroken when a new Master arrives at the temple: a man to whom Morgan is immediately drawn both mentally and physically, a man who is strikingly familiar... yet utterly alien.

Year of the Ram is a fully-fleshed novel, approximately 97000 words, with a focus on the love story and romance angle. Set against a science fiction milieu, it explores the infinite possibilities of the human and alien heart. Sexual content is explicit, though is not the primary focus of the novel.

For those who like a romance that forces its characters to contemplate the ecstasies and the agonies of love... you will enjoy *Year of the Ram*.

**Also available in paperback on Amazon,
or order from your favorite bookseller.**

All of our titles are available directly from our website, on Amazon, or may be ordered from most booksellers. Thanks for reading us!

Eye Scry Publications
A Visionary Publishing Company
www.eyescrypublications.com

www.ingramcontent.com/pod-product-compliance
Lightning Source LLC
Chambersburg PA
CBHW020326260626
47156CB00004B/1402